The
Jacob Maresbeth
Chronicles

Chronicle 1:
HIGH STAKES

HIGH STAKES

Brandy Schillace

COOPERATIVE TRADE

ADVANCE PRAISE FOR HIGH STAKES

JACOB MARESBETH ISN'T THE OVERLY SEXY, OVERLY PERfect, brooding vampire we've come to know. He's a real teenage boy, with all the insecurities and flaws that come with it. And, in my opinion, that just makes him all the more appealing. Jacob is certainly a character you enjoy spending time with, and want to root for.

High Stakes was a thoroughly enjoyable read from beginning to end. Schillace gives us a powerful debut, with a strong and an entertaining voice. The story was funny and sweet, but also suspenseful. At the end of this brief and brisk story, I was left wanting more. I can't wait for more Jacob Maresbeth, and more novels by Brandy Schillace.

—Sharon Bayliss, author of *The Charge*

IN *HIGH STAKES*, BRANDY SCHILLACE GIVES US A REFRESHING take on the teen vampire novel. Blending humor, intriguing characters, and some unexpected twists, she has created an entertaining read and a quirky new hero who will appeal to those thirsting for intelligent young adult fiction. I look forward to reading more Jacob Maresbeth stories. Recommended.

— David B. Coe/D.B. Jackson, author of the *Thieftaker Chronicles*

HIGH STAKES IS A FUNNY, ENJOYABLE READ, AND JACOB Maresbeth is an endearing character.

—Nina Post, author of *Zaanics Deceit*

COOPERATIVE TRADE
an imprint of Cooperative Press

HIGH STAKES
Volume 1 of The Jacob Maresbeth Chronicles
ISBN 13: 978-1-937513-44-3
First Edition
Published by Cooperative Press Trade, an imprint of Cooperative Press
www.cooperativetrade.com

Text © 2014, Brandy Schillace
Cover art © 2014, Brandy Schillace
All rights reserved.

Every effort has been made to ensure that all the information in this book is accurate at the time of publication. Cooperative Press neither endorses nor guarantees the content of external links referenced in this book. All business names, trademarks and product names used within the text are the property of their respective owners.

This novel is a work of fiction. All characters are imaginary and any resemblances to actual persons, either living or dead, is entirely coincidental.

For information about licensing, custom editions, special sales, or academic/corporate purchases, please contact Cooperative Press:
info@cooperativepress.com or
13000 Athens Ave C288, Lakewood, OH 44107 USA

No part of this book may be reproduced in any form, except brief excerpts for the purpose of review, without prior written permission of the publisher. Thank you for respecting our copyright.

Join the Cooperative Press Trade email list at
http://eepurl.com/DS-m1

Contents

Chapter 1 1

Chapter 2 11

Chapter 3 23

Chapter 4 33

Chapter 5 43

Chapter 6 55

Chapter 7 67

Chapter 8 85

Chapter 9 93

Chapter 10 103

Chapter 11 111

Chapter 12 119

For the Jacob Maresbeths everywhere:
The dead don't travel nearly as fast as the living.

Chapter 1

It was not a dark and stormy night. Actually, it was a hot, sticky June about a quarter past one—but balmy, blue skies don't help much when you're getting very bad news.

See, I live in Newport News, Virginia. That's not the bad news. How could it be? The trouble is not my town—it's my aunt. *Sylvia*. (Make sure you emphasize the first syllable...a fake British accent helps.) Aunt Syl is an English professor, which is bad enough. I don't want to be mean-spirited, but reading about dead white dudes does weird things to your brain. And maybe to your face, too; she has these big owl eyes and bigger owl glasses, the better to see old print with, I guess. But her greatest fault is probably the fact that she lives in Cleveland, Ohio. If you've never heard of it, I should explain that it's not a hot vacation spot ... in much the same way that Death Valley isn't selling out for honeymooners.

"Cleveland," I muttered, because I was lying on my bed with a pillow over my face at the time.

"Cleveland," my dad repeated. He was leaning over the large, rolling cooler on the floor and counting shiny, metallic bags. "It's … well.… It's where you're going."

He shrugged, and the total lack of enthusiasm was not helping me at all.

"Why do I have to do this?" I asked, sitting up and staring at the top of his bald head. "There's nothing to do there."

"There's plenty to do."

"Like what? Swim in Lake Erie? They set their own river on fire, Dad. And besides, you don't have to go—Mom's not even going!" Yes. I was whining. No, it wasn't working.

"Look, Jake," he sat down on his haunches. "It's just two weeks. You and Lizzy will have a great time—and besides, your aunt really looks forward to it."

"You know what's gonna happen, right?" I asked. "She's gonna give me the death watch. She'll be analyzing me and crap like that!"

You have to understand—Aunt Syl is like a medical microscope, and I've had about enough of that in my life.

"She won't," Dad insisted. But of course that was a lie … and lying is wrong.… "Well, OK, she will," he corrected. "But Jake, she's been doing that to you for years. It can't hurt you, can it?"

Hurt, no. Annoy and belittle, yes. I always come away from her house feeling like a sickly toddler.

"Why can't Lizzy just go by herself?"

"Jake, be nice. Now, I've told her not to cook for you—and I've packed enough of the bags for you to get by on and then some just in case." He tussled my hair. "Besides, Lizzy will be there, so she can draw fire if necessary."

"Oh yay, Lizzy to the rescue," I grumbled, slumping down on the bed again. Lizzy is my sister—my younger sister. But for some reason everyone thinks I need *her* to take care of *me*, as if I'd make a mess out of my already bizarre life without her help.

"Yes, Lizzy to the rescue," said Lizzy, who'd just entered my room without permission. Again. "Because you're a raging dork. Mom says lunch is ready, by the way."

"Just a second," my father pointed to the bags and did some mental calculation. "Thirty-six. Is that right?"

"Geez, Dad, I'm not staying forever," I argued. "I only need one of those a day—if that."

"Whatever," Lizzy rolled her eyes. "You eat twice as much as that when you feel all whiny and depressed."

"I do not!" I insisted, which was a total lie. Who doesn't over-eat when they're bored to tears?

"Are you three coming or not?" my mother asked, swinging the door open—and yes, now all of them were in my room, looking through my packing.

My mother has this way of arching her eyebrows; it's hard to explain, but it's like a whole sentence: "That's all you're sending with him?"

"Isn't thirty-six right for two weeks?" My dad asked (he's pretty good at reading eyebrows).

"Thirty-six!" she crossed her arms. "You know he overeats when he's depressed."

"Excuse me," I interrupted. "I am still here—could we not talk about me in the third person?"

This, you might have guessed, had practically no effect whatsoever.

"What, forty? Forty-two?" my dad asked.

"We could ask the blood-mobile to stop by," Lizzy snorted with entirely too much sarcasm.

"Lizzy, really!" My mother snapped. "Be nice to your brother."

Lizzy just shrugged and picked up a weird-looking instrument from the cooler's side compartment.

"What's this supposed to be?" she asked. I blinked at it—for some reason I hadn't noticed it among the other piles of junk I had to take with me.

"Is that a—a needle?" I asked. I hate needles. And other pointy objects.

Lizzy tossed her ponytail and then proceeded to point the syringe at me. It was attached to several hoses of some sort.

"It's a portable transfusion kit," my father said. "Don't break it; it's the only one I could find on short notice."

Lizzy actually laughed until she snorted.

"Transfusion! Oh come on, Dad, he's a *vampire*!" she said.

"I am not!" I yelled, throwing a pillow at her. "Dad!"

"He is *not* a vampire," my father repeated. "He's epilemic. You all know the terminology."

Lizzy cleared her throat.

"Epilemic," she began, performing like it was a spelling bee. "Aberration of the neurological dysfunction epilepsy, characterized by brain malfunction, manifested as episodic impairment and psychic disturbances, complicated by hemolytic anemia. Disease of unknown origin, first discovered by Franklyn Maresbeth, Newport News Medical, central campus."

"That's disturbances of brain function, not brain *malfunction*," my dad—the honored Franklyn Maresbeth himself—corrected. "But very, very good."

"Show off," I muttered, and Lizzy punched me in the shoulder.

"Whatever. And your brain *is* dysfunctional."

"Shut up, would you?" I asked. "There's nothing wrong with my brain."

"Yeah? Can *you* recite it?" She stared me down, knowing very well that I hadn't bothered to memorize it. "See?" she added with a wink. "Dysfunctional—vampire."

I scowled at her, but there wasn't much point in arguing. Not with Lizzy. Besides, it's a little true—sort of. I mean, I'm sixteen, not six-hundred. I don't turn into a bat. I don't go ransacking the neighborhood, and, though it would be *nice*, I'm *not* irresistibly attractive to the opposite sex. I'm just a tall, skinny blond kid with a doctor-dad and a blood disorder.

But let's face it, consuming raw blood instead of cheeseburgers kind of gets you noticed, and not in a good way. So Lizzy calls it vampirism and Dad calls it epilemia. I don't actually care so long as I'm more or less supplied with the basic necessities. You should see the basement cooler. I don't know what sort of deal my dad worked out with the hospital (helps, I guess, that he's bosom buddies with the Executive Director), but faking sick is better than being turned into some sort of ongoing vampire medical experiment. Or worse, getting burned at the stake. I've seen the movies; my team doesn't usually win.

The trouble is, faking sick is hard to do when you are so incredibly *healthy*. And Lizzy, who is the family actress, will tell you that I can't act to save my life. Literally. And *that's* why this two-week trip was causing such a fuss. It was the first time Lizzy and I were going to see Aunt Syl without my parents around to run interference.

And frankly, it didn't seem worth the effort to *me*.

"We could just cancel the trip, you know," I said, interrupting an ongoing conversation about—well, me.

"Jake, you're going. I'll get ten more from the cooler after lunch and bring them up," my mother was saying.

My dad nodded agreement.

"Son, make sure you keep that thing plugged in," he said, referring to the cooler. "Now, go wash up."

I heaved a sigh. I never seem to get my way around here. Even about mealtime. I don't actually *eat* with my family; I haven't touched solids since I was eight, so even if I wasn't "allergic" to everything (as my aunt believes), I probably don't have much of a digestive system left anyhow. Still, there are some family rituals you don't get out of, so I plugged the refrig-o-mat into the wall outlet and hustled to join everyone else. Aunt Syl was set to arrive around nine that night; she was staying in the downstairs guest room so that we could all get a "fresh early start" the next morning.

And of course, being me, mornings are not my thing.

Actually, mornings are so not my thing that I don't remember much about the beginning of the trip north. I more or less woke up in the back seat of Aunt Syl's car somewhere north of Warrenton, Virginia, on Highway 66.

"Er?" I mumbled. "Where are we?"

"About six hours away, now," Aunt Syl said cheerfully. Cheerful is her basic disposition, really. "Are you feeling quite well? We could stop if you feel the least bit fatigued—or ailing—or ill-at-ease. Are you comfortable? Tired?"

I blinked. Correction: cheerful and *wordy*.

"Fine," I said, clearing my throat.

"Throat tickle? I have lozenges, you know—your father didn't mention a throat tickle. Is it symptomatic?" She was staring at me through the rear-view mirror, the chain of her rimmed glasses bouncing around and blinding me with reflected sunlight. So, given that and the fact that I'd woken up 45 seconds earlier, I just sat there with my mouth open.

"He does that when he wakes up, you know," Lizzy said. "It's *so* difficult for him. He's terribly slow in the head when he wakes up."

I gritted my teeth and prepared to defend myself, but of course I *am* a little slow when I first wake up, so that didn't go very well.

"It's—I'm—what?" was all I could do.

"See?" Lizzy said, casting a malicious grin at me over her shoulder. I kind of hate her, a little. "Now, what were you saying about the theater?"

"Oh, you will *truly* love it!" Aunt Syl winked one of her big owl-eyes and gave the steering wheel a little slap. "*Com-plete-ly* renovated! Gorgeous frescoes! Absolutely astonishing work!"

I could tell Lizzy was starting to salivate. She's got acting on the brain, for some reason. I suppose it's only natural since she's a drama queen to begin with.

"And we'll go to the plays?" she asked, forgetting to act cool and looking for a minute like she really was just a fourteen-year-old theater geek.

"Certainly we will! The Shakespeare festival is just kicking off! But that is hardly the pinnacle of your entertainment for the season! I have *quite* a surprise for you, Lizzy dear! Quite!"

Aunt Syl gave her head a little shake, making her unruly brownish-red curls boing all over. I sometimes can't believe she and my mother are in the same family.... How do a pale, sleek blond and a frazzly, freckled redhead end up sisters, I want to know? And how come my mother—the one with real sense in my opinion—isn't the one with a PhD?

"A surprise?" Lizzy asked, fiddling with the air-conditioning vent. "What could be better than tickets to the shows?"

My aunt gave a little shiver of—I don't know, happiness, let's say—and leaned toward Lizzy.

"How would you like to be *in* a play? Mmmm?" Uh-oh, I thought. Lizzy's gonna have a heart attack.

"*In* a play? Really?" Lizzy's normally got a narrow I-know-more-than-you expression, but her eyes were almost as big as Syl's for a minute. My aunt leaned back with a satisfied thump (and a lot of clinking, since it shuffled all of her various beads and bangles).

"Yes, really. As an extra, of course, and I know that isn't terribly flattering by itself. But I do have one little surprise left!"

I rolled my eyes. No one ever has surprises for *me*, you'll notice ... probably afraid I'd have some sort of fit. Of course, at the moment, Lizzy looked like she might have one herself if Aunt Syl didn't quit beating around the bush.

"Another—?" She asked, leaning forward as if proximity would wheedle it out.

"I have enrolled you in an acting class! A *college* class, Lizzy dear, with a gifted actor and head of the theater department!"

"Aunt Syl—Oh! *Thanks* so much, it's—" Lizzy started.

"It starts in two weeks!" Aunt Syl interrupted with another wheel slap. And now, of course, I started seeing a potential problem.

"Uh, Aunt Syl?" I ventured. "We're sort of leaving in two weeks."

"Oh I know, but that's easy enough to remedy, is it not? How wonderful! You can both stay with me for *four* weeks! That way Lizzy can play a part in a real stage production, and then have the benefit of true theater instruction!"

She seemed very pleased that this had rhymed.

"And don't worry Jacob," she continued. "I promise you and I will have a capital time!"

I think I was paralyzed at the suggestion ... even though the thought of playing an invalid in boring, stupid Cleveland for my over-zealous aunt was almost incentive enough to jump out of a moving car. Lizzy recovered a little more quickly.

"Oh—well, *thank* you very much," she said a little tightly. "Mom and Dad will surely want to hear all about this. Don't you think so, Jake?"

Oh, I did indeed.

Chapter 2

AS IT HAPPENS, MY PARENTS WERE *VERY* INTERESTED IN Aunt Syl's plan—particularly the fact that she didn't think it required parental permission. It was *her* time and money, after all, and didn't they want Lizzy's acting aspirations to be "efficacious, productive, and sufficiently well-grounded?" It might almost have been a humorous phone call if my fate weren't depending on it. Dad had packed almost enough of the blood-bags for four weeks, but thankfully he sympathized with the psychological damage that additional visit time would cause me. (Besides, its beach season in Newport News, and I was missing it).

Lizzy was all up for the challenge, of course, since Aunt Sylvia was her new favorite person, but Dad promised to come get me at the end of week two. Aunt Syl would drive Lizzy back up after classes were over. Problem solved. Sort of; I still had to put up with my aunt's fussing and fluttering around me like a big well-meaning bird.

"You had better get early to bed, Jacob dear," she said, poising over me with a teapot. "More herbal?"

"Er, no, thanks," I said. I can drink tea and most other water-based fluids. But I don't really like it much, and whatever Aunt Syl was brewing smelled and tasted pretty awful.

"Sure? It's arrowroot and honeywort—very cleansing!"

"Thanks, but I feel pretty clean already," I said, trying to smile like I meant it. Lizzy was sitting across the room from me, hiding her face in a magazine and trying not to laugh. Which wasn't helping much. I decided "early to bed" was as good an idea as any, so I faked a yawn. My aunt, who watches my every move anyway, seemed to take the hint.

"Very good, very good—off to bed with you, then," she said, shooing me towards the big front stairs.

My room is at the top of the steps, the one with blue carpet and denim curtains. You know, "boy's" colors. Lizzy's is some shade of rose or pink.... Aunt Syl needs a life so bad it hurts.

"Now, Jake," she was saying (because she'd followed me up the stairs, of course), "there are extra towels in the linen closet. I left a few little things out for you to look at ... brochures, you know. Summer classes don't begin for two weeks, but—oh, *there* you are!"

Aunt Syl stopped in mid-sentence to swish her two cats, Byron and Shelley, off my bed. In movies, vampires always get wolves and bats. Me, I attract cats. The dumb things *love* me.

"Just look at them, so delighted to see you! Feline felicity!" My aunt tittered to herself as the cats did figure-eights around my legs.

"Er—you were saying?" I asked, trying not to step on anyone.

"Ah, yes! I have to take Lizzy to orientation tomorrow; then I have to prepare for my own summer classes. I am *so* sorry you'll be here all alone, but I *promise* we'll be back by 2:00. I know the week might be a bit slow, but don't you trouble yourself! We'll have a mad, dashing time this weekend!"

"Great. That's—what, the play, right?" I asked. Then I faked another yawn, hoping she'd chalk up my lack of enthusiasm to lack of sleep.

"*Précisément*!" she said. Yes, not content to throw the English dictionary at you, she gets French in there, too. She's a mean Scrabble player.

"Right—well—I'll just—" But what I was "just" doing was falling over a fat cat. I managed to catch hold of the dresser and swing myself over the both of them and onto the other side of the bed.

But that's bad. My aunt's eyes got as big as dinner plates, making me wish I'd just fallen over. See, I'm not exactly coordinated most of the time, but I get a little rush of energy in the evening… something that I—as an "invalid" and all—am not supposed to have.

"Luck?" I said lamely.

"You young men, all acrobats I suppose! Well," she straightened her bangles and checked her watch. "You *will* tell me if you need anything? Mmm? See, I left a bell here in case there's an emergency in the night!"

"Thank you, Aunt Syl," I said grimacing.

"And I know you keep your own special food—but *if* you want anything, even a wee snack?"

"I promised Dad no snacks," I said, crossing my heart.

"Quite right, of course," she said with a little shrug and finally (thankfully) headed for the door. "Oh, one more thing, dear. I *do* have a graduate student or two coming here tomorrow. They're doing annotations for me in the library, but don't be alarmed! They're quite safe and quiet as church mice!"

With that, she bobbed on down the steps again, and I let out a sigh I hadn't realized I'd been holding in. *This was going to be such a loooong two weeks,* I thought. *I have a cow-bell alarm system and an aunt who thinks I'm afraid of her graduate students.* Have you ever met a graduate student? Apparently, to be really good at it, you have to hate sleep, food, and social life, and enjoy reading books by people who are now dead. My aunt's previous graduate assistant, Leonard, was fidgety and morose and apparently suffering from malnutrition. He always reminded me of a melancholy squirrel. These are *not* people who inspire fear.

"Scoot, cat," I said to Shelley, who was getting her orange fur all over my pants. I checked to see that conversation was happening downstairs and then shut and locked the door. It was dinnertime, after all, and I didn't need to go freaking anybody out. I'd plugged the cooler in under the window so I could keep the thing shoved between the bed and the wall. I wasn't exactly hiding it; my aunt knew that I brought blood "transfusion" supplies with me, and I had an assortment of health-food looking crap in the top compartment as a screen. It's just that serious inspection would make it clear there was more blood than food in there, and I'm not so good at fielding questions. I unbuttoned the flap and opened the hard case of the cooler, and suddenly life seemed a little brighter. Forty-five tidy little packages, like deep red juice boxes. Dad's design, bless him. I picked one up, nipped the top off, and sucked it down so fast I didn't really taste it.... Not that they taste terribly interesting, but I've grown rather fond.

Forty-four left. You'd think I was staying forever. Which meant, really, there was no reason why I couldn't have *another* one.... So I did. And (I hate to admit it) one more after that. I wasn't even hungry, but the stuff calms me, and I figured that, after the day I'd had, I deserved a treat. Besides, it helped me face the second dilemma of the evening: I have nocturnal tendencies, it was only nine o'clock, and there's no TV upstairs. Lucky for me, an over-full tank tends to induce sleepiness.

I propped myself up with pillows with a stack of "Great Things about Cleveland" pamphlets and my favorite notebook. Yes, *note*book—not *net*book. I got my dad's hand-me-down computer last year, but I like my spiral-bound-flip-top legal pad just fine. I'm not anti-tech or anything. It's just that since I was five, I've always wanted to be a reporter. Not a fireman (fire? really?). Not a doctor (had enough of hospitals). A journalist. And in my opinion, *real* journalists carry notebooks. Don't have to plug it in. Just have to write in it.

I flipped it open to the last entry, but that one wasn't even mine. It was Henry's: *Dude, tell the college chicks I said hi!* I smirked. Henry's my best friend, but he has these delusions about visiting my college-professor-aunt. The town is not crawling with sorority hotties; it's summer, for one thing, and besides, my aunt prefers weirdo grad students. I flipped the page and clicked the ballpoint: *Monday, June 8th: Arrived. Unpacked. Yee-haw.* The Cleveland brochures didn't inspire much more than that, though I could probably write up some sort of "summer travel" spot for the school paper. But who would read it? Stinky city with stinky lake, empty campus, twitchy research assistant. Exciting stuff. I dumped the pamphlets on the floor and switched off the light. I then proceeded to stare broodingly at the ceiling until I fell asleep.

When I woke up the next morning (11 am is still morning), however, I found I could not move. It wasn't paralysis. It was cat-love. I'd been trapped Gulliver-style by Byron and Shelley, who'd managed to tuck themselves into the blanket on either side.

"Off, off already!" I said, wriggling loose and knocking Byron onto the floor. He protested but took the hint; Shelley just dug her claws into the bedspread so I had to leave her there. I managed to find my toiletry bag and then slogged into the bathroom.

Thankfully, I have my own bathroom at Syl's. You know, because I'm sickly and "enervated" or whatever she thinks about me. If the medicine cabinet is any indication, she thinks *a lot* about me. Lozenges with zinc in them... a bunch of herbal supplements for everything from night sweats to diarrhea. There was even some sort of medicated soap stuff next to my washcloth. I wrinkled my nose—it's not like I have leprosy or something (though to Syl, that would be like Christmas). Lizzy's room is not decked out like a drug store; I checked. I'm just lucky that way.

The sun was high by the time I got out of the shower, but it wasn't all that warm, frankly. (When *does* it get warm in Cleveland, I wonder?) I opted for long sleeves, brushed my teeth, and then headed downstairs to occupy myself until Syl and Lizzy got home.

Occupy yourself. That's one of my mother's favorites. And trust me, you'd better do it because she can think of *all kinds* of things to occupy you with. On the bright side, Lizzy and I have learned to be great at self-amusement, and Aunt Syl's house actually has plenty to offer. It's got its own library (if you're into that), a pool table and a pretty serious entertainment system in the den. I peeked out the front room window; the sun was getting blocked by thick-looking rain clouds, so I felt more or less guilt-free about deciding on TV. Aunt Syl only gets basic cable, but she's a film buff with more than two hundred titles ... lots of them black and white. Bela Lugosi is a big favorite (yay, more vampires that get staked) but she also has a bunch of Bogart films, so I stretched, yawned, and headed for the library to collect them.

And then, I think I died.

At least, my heart stopped for a minute. Why? Because I had just seen an angel.

The library is a big room with tall windows and Victorian-style furniture; the bookshelves are on one end, and on the other is a low table where Aunt Syl keeps her current projects spread out. There, in a little pool of light from the window, was a girl. Not just a girl, either. A *woman*-girl. The sun broke through the clouds to shine on her hair, which was golden and tied in a braid so thick it looked like dock-rope. She was leaning over the table when I entered, but she turned—very slowly—and looked up at me. A round face, peaked at the chin like an acorn, with the most utterly fascinating eyes. Meanwhile, I stood there with my mouth open.

"I am sorry? Can I help?" She asked with a gently rolling accent that I'd never heard before.

"I—you—you're not Leonard," I stuttered. This was not even remotely Bogart, incidentally. More like Woody Allen on a bad day.

"I am not," she smiled and put her book down. "I am Zsòfia."

"Sophia?" I asked stupidly.

"No, no—Zsa, Zsa," she puckered her lips as she said it, make a breathy soft "g" sound, "Zsòfia."

I swallowed and looked for a place to sit before my legs melted.

"Zsòfia," I repeated. "It's wonderful!—to meet you, I mean...." (I cringe to write this.) "You're, ah, not from around here?" (I cringe to write that, too.)

"No, not at all. I am from Hungary. You are Jacob, yes?" She tucked a pen behind her ear, and I gulped air like a fish on land.

"Yeah—Jacob Maresbeth. Aunt Syl is my, oh—well, my aunt." I was mentally smacking myself as a reminder to do it for real later ... this was not cool. This was the *opposite* of cool.

"She tells me about you and your sister. Are you playing?" she asked.

"Playing?" I sure hoped not.

"I am sorry—are you *acting* in the play? Your sister, she is an actress."

"Oh, no—I mean, yes, she is. But I'm not. I write," I said, not without a little hint of returning pride. Okay, it's not Pulitzer material, but I have the notebook and I *do* write things in it. Zsòfia nodded.

"That is right! You are the journalist, I remember. I write as well, you see," she indicated the scattered note cards and other materials. "But it is a dissertation."

Now, I had no idea what a dissertation was, but I wasn't about to admit that.

"Oh?" I asked, praying my voice wouldn't crack as it still does sometimes. "What's it about?"

"You would not be interested," she said, shaking her head (and making that wonderful braid bounce around). "It is all work, work, research, and history."

"No, really! I would love to hear about it!" I said, which was true, because I could listen to her voice all day. She could be telling me the history of plywood for all I cared.

"It tells something about my country. Hungary lies in the Carpathian Basin of central Europe. Do you know where that is?" she asked.

I shook my head and then went back to staring.

"It is not far from Romania, you see—the region of Transylvania, what we call *Erdély* in Hungarian."

"Transylvania?" I started.

"Yes, and this region was once part of Hungary, before the 1500s. It is a very beautiful place, and very mountainous," she said, still smiling. I relaxed a little.

"So, ah, your dissertation is about the mountains there?"

"No, no," Zsòfia shrugged her pretty shoulders and looked back to her work. "It is about vampires."

She said this so nonchalantly that for a minute it didn't totally register. When it did, I'm afraid I made a little chirping sound.

"Vampires? Like, um—really?" I squeaked. She nodded.

"Your aunt, she likes the *vámpír* very much, do you know? She has the films for *Dracula*, and Bela Lugosi, he was a Hungarian." She took the pen from her ear and marked something in her notebook. Then she looked back at me. "The vampire in film and literature. That is my dissertation; I study the history of the myth in my country and in the world."

And suddenly I felt a little bit dumb.

"Oh. Yeah. Yeah?" I said. Frankly, I read a fair bit of vampire lore myself, for obvious reasons. "Well that sounds interesting. I bet lots of people want to know about that."

"Not so many," she sighed. "They want to read fiction, they don't want to know its history."

"I do!" I said emphatically. "I *love* history!"

"Truly?" she asked, blinking her dark eyes. "I am very much pleased. We can talk about it sometime maybe. But I must do your aunt's notes, now."

She was, after all, working. And though it was very polite, it was more or less a send-off. I felt a prickly sensation run down my spine and thanked my stars that I'm not capable of blushing. Or not visibly, anyway.

"Right. Right, well—I'll just be, around," I stood up and inched my way out of the room.

"Goodbye, Jacob Maresbeth," she said, but she wasn't looking in my direction anymore. She was nosing through Aunt Syl's notes again, oblivious to the teenage dork who had just interrupted her studies. I squeezed around the corner and set about smacking myself in earnest.... I'd forgotten the video in my shock and was absolutely *not* man enough to go back and get it. And so, I wandered out on the porch instead, and sat there moony and star-struck until my aunt and sister got home.

Chapter 3

Zsòfia left around 1:30, exiting through the back door—meaning I didn't actually see her off. I just heard the ring of her bicycle bell as she rolled down the tree-lined street, the dock-rope braid swaying as she pedaled. She wasn't looking, but I waved goodbye, and then forgot to put my arm down until my fingers got tingly. I also forgot to quit staring until she'd been gone about ten minutes. I swear, it was like being under a spell or something. Except I liked it. A lot. And, in the interest of getting more of it, I descended on my aunt like a ravenous dog when she got home.

"But who *is* she??" I demanded, leaning on the back of a dining chair. My aunt was in the thick of dinner preparations—which is sort of demanding on someone who usually eats frozen-health-food-for-one (the equivalent, I think, of grass and dirt).

"My research assistant, you silly boy." She tasted a sauce of some kind and flipped a page in her cookbook. "You remember Leonard?"

"*She* is not Leonard," I insisted, and Lizzy sidled up to punch me in the shoulder.

"What, you crushing on somebody already?" she asked, as if the experience of Zsòfia could be compared to anything so stupid.

"No!—she's, I don't know—have you seen her yet?" I stammered. "She's *Hungarian*."

"So?" Lizzy asked, and I decided to ignore her and turned my attention back to Aunt Syl.

"How did she end up *here*, in Cleveland?"

"She's from Budapest, originally, though her father lives in Krakow, Poland," Aunt Syl said, sliding by with plates (just two of them). "She studied first at Edinburgh—"

"Right. But why is she *here*?" I asked. My aunt set the table and blinked owl-eyes at me.

"Why not?"

"Yeah, Jakey, why not?" Lizzy repeated, grinning like the she-devil she is. How was I supposed to explain that Cleveland was—to put it nicely—a bit of a step down?

"Well, it's a long way, isn't it?" I asked. It was a good save. Lizzy looked disappointed.

"It is, indeed—careful, careful, this is hot, Jacob!" Aunt Syl set down a crock pot that I was *miles* away from, shooing me as if I was about to stick my hand in there or something. "She has been tracking down some data at the medical library. And, of course, she is a wonderful student. Top of her class."

"Top of her class," I repeated out loud, though I hadn't meant to.

"What's she doing at the medical library?" Lizzy asked, sitting down at the long table. My aunt's dining room is more of a hallway, long and skinny between the kitchen and the big front room. I slid around the back to make room for Syl and the salad.

"Dissertations are complicated things!" Syl said, sitting—and for once, I sat, too. I normally try not to join these little dining parties, but I actually wanted to figure out what a dissertation was.

"She is working on vampires in culture, so she looks at psychology, medicine, literature, film. It's quite an interesting process! Why, some graduate students compile data for *years*!"

"She'll be here for *years*?" I asked. "Like, every summer?"

"It's certainly possible," my aunt nodded happily.

"And she'll be here, as your assistant? For years?"

It was at this point that Lizzy started giggling.

"What, you think you might eventually be old enough to ask her out?" she laughed. Lizzy has this funny way of sucking the fun out of life. She would have made a much better vampire than me.

"Wha—no—I was just. Curious." I started fiddling with the bread knife. I think I was trying to trace the tablecloth pattern. Or mentally performing a lobotomy on my sister. Something like that.

"Well, Jacob, curiosity is a *very* good thing," Aunt Syl said, smiling at me like I was four years old. "I'm sure it passes the time when you're unwell. By the way, did you see I put digestive aids in your cabinet? For irritable bowels, you know."

Yes. She actually said that.

Yes, my sister almost imploded from trying not to laugh.

Yes, I cut myself with the stupid bread knife.

This last bit, however, was a crisis of a different nature. First, I can't even begin to describe what Aunt Syl's reaction to blood is. Maybe she missed her calling—maybe she should have gone MD instead of PhD. She's got some sort of obsession with doctoring, and she saves it up all year just for me. Naturally, I couldn't let her see that I'd been careless enough to cut my thumb (and pretty deeply at that). But there's another reason.

"Ah—excuse me," I said, making a fist over the wound and backing away from the table.

"Why, Jake! What's the matter!" My aunt was nearly out of her seat again, but Lizzy seemed to put the pieces together (spotting the red dots on the knife helped).

"Oh, well, it's his digestion problem," she said unhelpfully. I scowled at her, but really, I had bigger problems.

I scooted out of the dining room, my fist behind my back. Aunt Syl had resumed her seat and Lizzy had managed to get hold of and clean the bloodied knife before she saw it. As soon as I was out of sight, I had another look at the thing: I'd managed to slice it horizontally, and a trickle of blood had escaped to run towards my elbow.

"Crap, crap," I grunted, slipping into the first floor bathroom. I managed to catch the drip before it got on my sleeves. Then, I waited. It took about seven minutes. In that time, the cut had closed back up without even a scar ... which almost beats my busted knuckle record from last fall.

My dad calls it *exceler curatio*, which is some fancy Latin phrase for fast healing. Apparently they do studies on mice with fast-healer genes. I'm a lot bigger than a mouse, and I heal a lot faster. Beyond that I don't know a whole lot about it. Lizzy thinks we should try cutting one of my toes off to see it if grows back, mutant style. (She's loving like that.) Me, I'd like to think of it as a gift—except it's ruined a lot of my high school career. Why? Because my mother refuses to let me play sports. Why? Glad you asked. I ask *every year*. But since this whole quick-healing deal is not part of the Maresbeth "official" description, I'm not supposed to let people know about it. My mother apparently thinks it would be hard to explain a disappearing abrasion to the football coach. If it was my dad, I could probably work out a compromise. But Mother Maresbeth is like a pit bull. If she gets hold of an idea, she's not letting go of it. Period.

I licked my palm (no reason to waste it) and washed up. Then, though it killed me to do it, I flushed the toilet for cover. The only good side to this mess was that Aunt Syl *might* stop making remarks about my bathroom habits. Apparently the mere suggestion of digestive malfunction sends me running to the toilet.

I hate my life sometimes.

When I got back to the table, they were partway through casserole. It was painful, the look of pity Aunt Syl was giving me, but I just *had* to find out more about Zsòfia.

"Ahem," I said, trying to act casual. "What did I miss?"

Lizzy rested her chin on her hand and peered at me ever-so-sweetly.

"Well, Zsòfia is way too old for you—and she's got a crush on someone else, anyway."

"Oh. Sure," I said—at least I think I said that. I couldn't hear myself because my heart had just exploded with a deafening bang. Zsòfia with someone else was horrifying enough—but I had just thought of something worse.

"Not Leonard. Please."

"Oh, heavens!" Aunt Syl gave herself a little hug and grinned at me. "Hardly her type, I think. Lizzy is having you—what do they say? Over a barrel? It's Bela Lugosi!"

"Wait—the actor?" I asked.

"Indeed! Zsòfia quite pines for him! Has seen every film, I'm quite sure. Many of them twice. Or thrice!"

I restarted my heart. Zsòfia: not dating. Loves Bela Lugosi. It was only then that I had a chance to attend to the second part of my aunt's comment. Frankly, does *anyone* say "over a barrel"? I sometimes wonder what century she lives in....

"So she likes movies," I said, glaring at Lizzy. "I like movies. What else does she like?"

My aunt tilted her head a little, unbalancing her bangles.

"You know, my dear, she keeps very much to herself. It must be difficult adjusting to another university; she left the one in Edinburgh only a year ago. But she is a *most* excellent assistant, and really quite charming. Perhaps you can keep her company when she's here."

Okay, I've never been super fond of Aunt Syl, but right now I could have kissed the woman.

"Sure. I mean, you know, why not?" I said. Translation: *Thank you, Lord Jesus, his saints, and angels, and anyone else listening up there, amen.*

My aunt winked at me and then started clearing the dishes away. Meanwhile, I was getting the stink-eye from my sister.

"Are you that dumb?" she asked.

"What's the matter? For once there's a *girl* research assistant. So what."

"So what? You idiot. First, she's not into you."

"You don't know that."

Lizzy raised her eyebrows in a pretty good rendition of our mother. Only my sister's version said: *don't make me tell you what a dork you are.*

"Go away," I said, heading for the stairs.

"Hold it, mister," Lizzy swung around the edge of the table and headed me off. "Listen, you big dummy, don't go drooling over Dracula-lover, alright? We don't know her. It's risky."

"What *are* you talking about?"

"News flash: *she's* not from around here! She's from *over there*," Lizzy said, pointing vaguely behind me.

"From the kitchen?" I asked. Lizzy leaned forward and gripped me by the front of my shirt.

"From *vampire* country!" she whispered.

"For the last time—I am *not* a vampire—"

"You drink blood," she hissed, and I grimaced.

"Stop it! *Dad* wouldn't let you talk like that!"

Lizzy let go of my shirt and crossed her arms. "Yeah? Well, Dad's not here, is he?"

"I can take care of myself," I snapped, and then I stomped up the stairs to—well, to drink blood.

There's just no getting around that.

I sat on the edge of the bed, scrunching my toes in the carpet and drinking down dinner number two (and three). My notepad was open on the comforter: *June 9th: Lizzy is a hateful brat.* Followed by ten pages trying to accurately describe Zsòfia's hair, eyes and accent—and one rather bad sketch. The trouble with Lizzy, though, is that she's sort of right ... so much of my life does seem to revolve around what I can and can't say about what I can and can't do. It's worse than annoying. If it weren't for Henry—who knows all about it, mostly due to an ill-advised attempt to become blood brothers when we were nine—I think I'd lose my mind. And of course, he wasn't there. So, I dug through my bag and produced my cell phone.

"Hey, Henry," I muttered when he picked up.

"Yo! What's happening, Jakey?"

"Nothing. Well, mostly nothing." I must have sounded pretty low. There was a pause as Henry switched ears.

"Syl's making you nuts, right?"

"Yup. And Lizzy."

"Yeah—she's hilarious," Henry laughed. I do not agree. But whatever. It was nice to hear a friendly voice. I described the disasters so far, and then went in for my real questions....

"So, do you know anything about Hungary?" I asked.

"Tons!" Henry said, and I admit this was a bit of a shock.

"Seriously?"

"Duh, Jake. I'm hungry all the time. Went wind-surfing today, and I'm starving!"

I thumped the phone against my forehead.

"No, Henry! The *country*! The country of Hungary!"

"Oh. Nope. Why?" he paused. "Dude, did you meet some chick from there or something?"

"Uh," I cleared my throat ... technically we *had* met. I'd "met" someone.

"Well, yeah," I said, grinning. "Graduate student."

"A graduate! Holy crap! That's like A-double-plus!"

All right. So I was letting Henry get the wrong end of the situation. So what? It felt great to be applauded for my as-yet-untried suaveness by someone who was spending *his* break wind surfing. It renewed my confidence. Tomorrow, I would be cool, and it would be awesome.

When I hung up, I pitched the empty container back in the cooler and slumped onto the pillows. *Zsòfia*. (I really liked saying her name.) She likes films. *Check*. She likes vampire stuff. *Check*. She likes mature-for-their-age high school boys...?

Man, I *seriously* hoped so.

Chapter 4

WEDNESDAY DAWNED CHEERY AND BRIGHT. I KNOW this because I actually set my alarm and got up at 9:00—I wanted to look well groomed and, you know, conscious, before Zsòfia got there. Unfortunately, this meant Lizzy and Syl were still bustling about.

"It's tonight! It's tonight!" Lizzy was doing the breakfast dishes for my aunt, crowing like a rooster.

"What's tonight?" I yawned, hunting through the cabinet for a coffee mug. I don't like tea, it's true, but I'm not sure I'd survive without coffee. Caffeine, apparently, works as well on me as anyone.

"Are you kidding? The play! *Midsummer Night's Dream!*"

"Whoa, whoa, whoa," I protested. "Syl said we didn't *have* to go till this weekend!"

"*Have* to go? Look, mister, you can keep your butt here for all *I* care," Lizzy tossed her head. "These are rehearsals. I'm going to be an extra in *Midsummer* on Saturday! Oh, I hope I can be a fairy!"

I blinked at her.

"Fairy," I repeated. I think I had planned to say something sarcastic, but my brain was just warming up—and anyway, Lizzy had just snapped me with the wet dish towel.

"Ouch! Why did you do that?!"

"Because you were thinking and nothing good ever comes from that. Yes, dork boy, a fairy. Like Puck."

"Puke."

"PUCK!"

"Ah, yes, indeed!" Aunt Syl had just shuffled into the kitchen, which was getting blindingly bright from the eastern window. "Puck, the trickster of the wood!"

My aunt was dressed in something like a drape tricked out with post-it notes and bits of notebook paper. The stuff sort of multiplies around her, I think.

"Puck serves Oberon, king of the fairies!" She explained with a wink.

"Wait, the fairies are guys?" This was a little weird for me, especially at 9 am. Syl didn't answer, though. She probably thought much more information would fry my brain cells. She just tussled my hair (everyone does, for some reason) and ushered Lizzy towards the front door.

"Now, Jacob, we'll pop back around five to pick you up; and *just in case*—I put a few snacks in the pantry for you."

"Aunt Syl, I promised Dad no—wait, you'll pick me up for *what*?"

"Well, you silly boy, you can't *walk* to the theater, can you?" Syl tut-tutted. "How else will you get to Lizzy's rehearsal?"

I could see from the gleam in Lizzy's eye that she'd planned this somehow.

"Ah—well, I'm not sure that—" I stuttered, but they were through the door already and onto the porch.

"Bye Jak-ey! See you toni-ight!" Lizzy sang and blew me a kiss like she was *just* an angel ... right before slamming the door in my face. She was not making happy marks in my sibling book, I can tell you. But to be honest, I had other things to think about; it was 9:45 and I had fifteen minutes to practice my cool.

So. Should I meet her at the door? Too obvious, I thought. But I didn't want to be lurking either.... I finally decided I would just be *in* the library when she got there, reading some suitably sexy and mature book. I mean, Syl's got a million of them in there—and besides, I knew *exactly* what to look for.

You would be really surprised how many biographies of Bela Lugosi there actually are. I was. I was not, however, surprised to find that my aunt owned *all* of them. Some didn't have covers anymore; that wouldn't work. I needed something nice and visible. I finally picked one with his photo on the front (and gory red letters). Next problem: looking cool. There's a long couch in there, but lying down just looks lazy. I tried the barcalounger, but the leather makes farting sounds when you move.... The only thing left was an old-looking armchair, and I was just trying to figure out the best possible way of getting into it (I'm sort of tall and its sort of small) when the front door rattled open.

Now, the front door faces into the hall, and the library is to the right. That meant I couldn't see the entrance, but it also meant I had only five seconds to throw myself into a reading posture. This did not work in my favor. I ended up with a leg over the side and an arm pinned behind my head—with the embarrassing consequence of one hand sort of flapping behind my left ear. I was also trying to hold the book up high enough for her to see it, so my elbow was just hanging out in midair. Sad to say, I probably looked like some sort of teenage origami experiment.

I heard the door click closed and the rustling of bags. A light step on the hall rug followed, and at this point my heart was beating so hard is almost hurt. (My arm and leg hurt, too, but I'd forgotten about them). I held my breath—and in another moment—

Leonard came walking into the room.

"Oh," he adjusted his glasses ... and I adjusted my attitude.

"Oh," I said back.

"I—that is—I thought Zsòfia would be, um, here," he stammered. And I hated him. A lot.

"Well. She isn't."

"No? Your aunt, er—she said—"

Leonard didn't finish. The back door had just jingled open, and he had some kind of seizure or something. It was like a twitch doing the wave. On the bright side, against the backdrop of this melancholy squirrel, I was bound to look pretty good.

"Hello!" Zsòfia entered the room like a shaft of light. Really. The sun was blazing through all the windows, and she was wearing sunshine yellow. "Why, Leonard, I did not think you would be here. Do you also annotate today?"

"Yes," said the twitch. "That is, no. I was picking up a book from Dr. Sylvia."

"Funny. Aunt Sylvia isn't here," I explained. Loudly. "I guess you'll have to go to her office."

Zsòfia now turned in my direction, all dimpled chin and dark eyes.

"Oh, Jacob! I did not see you!"

"Um, yeah. Just, you know. Reading," I lifted the book up. And then realized I was holding it upside down. "Er—I mean, I was. Earlier."

I righted the thing and tapped the cover. Zsòfia swept forward, her skirts rustling.

"Bela Lugosi! Yes, I have read that one myself—your aunt, she lent it to me!"

"Well, you know. He was," I flipped the book open somewhere in the middle and read the first thing I came across: "Er, the leading actor of the Royal National Theatre."

"Oh yes! But his acting career did not really happen until Germany. Did you know he played Shakespeare first?" She brushed past Leonard, who was polishing his glasses as though trying to put a hole through them. Clearly, he had been outclassed.

"Sure. I love Shakespeare," I lied.

"But he was not best at Shakespeare. He was best at Count Dracula!"

"Absolutely," I agreed. "I don't like Shakespeare nearly as much as Count Dracula."

"Me as well!" Zsòfia turned smiling eyes on Leonard. "Do you see the Bela Lugosi films?"

"The—no—well, I haven't."

Twitch, twitch.

"Dr. Sylvia, I think, has them all. She would let you see them."

"I haven't a television. Right now. I mean."

Twitch.

Leonard was sinking fast. I think I actually got two inches taller just sitting there. It was fantastic. Two Lugosi comments later, and he excused himself out the front door on the pretense of finding that book. Or maybe to go soak his head.

Unfortunately, that signaled the end of our conversation, too.

"You must tell me how you like this book," Zsòfia said, walking to that table near the far wall. "Now I must work."

"Sure," I sighed (uncontrollably). "Uh, I'll just finish reading. There's those other biographies, too."

"Mmmm," Zsòfia had a pen in her mouth. Her lips were just *so* pink....

"I've read about lots of film stars," I said—though I don't know why. Zsòfia nodded and looked at her work, and I started to sweat a little. *Don't be dumb, don't be dumb*....

"And vampires," I said. "I read about vampires."

Zsòfia put her pen down.

"About fictions. Many people read fictions."

"No, about history," I said, which is true. "Even the Greeks had myths about vampires."

Zsòfia looked at me for a long minute. (72 seconds. I counted.)

"Ambrogio," she said. "He was cursed by the sun god, Apollo. Did you learn this at high school?"

Now, for a minute, I'd been proud of that little factoid. But having high school mentioned sort of popped the balloon of happiness.

"Ah, no. I just like to do research," I said. Then I went out on a limb. "Just like you. Right?"

Zsòfia smiled at me. It was sort of indulgent, the kind of the smile my aunt gives me. But it was a smile, and I liked it.

"We will have to talk more when I am not working," she said. "I like to hear that you are interested."

She *liked* that I was *interested*. Liked. Interested. Naturally, I levitated for a minute or two. I also back-checked my mental record of every possible vampire thing I'd ever come across anywhere. If Lizzy knew, she'd have a canary. My dad wouldn't be too pleased, either, and my mother would have killed me. But it was *working*, and, after all, they weren't *there*.

For the rest of the week, I got dragged to absolutely every single rehearsal (every single night), but I also got to spend the afternoons in the library with Zsòfia (and Bela Lugosi and a stack of vampire legends). It made listening to Puke butchering the Queen's English almost bearable. It did not make Lizzy more bearable, though. She had gone absolutely ape over the acting gig and was making me crazy.

For one thing, she kept accusing me of not paying attention to the play she was in. Well, duh. Of course I wasn't. Not by Saturday anyhow, since I'd been dragged to the thing *four* times already. Luckily I have pretty amazing night vision, meaning I could still write in my notebook during rehearsals. Then, I'd managed to get out of Sunday's matinee by pretending to be "fatigued" after church. I will always hold a special place in my heart for "things going rotten in Denmark," since it meant Lizzy's play was over and I could finally quit going. Journal heading: *Monday, June 15th: Thank you, Hamlet.*

Lizzy still went, though. She and Syl were there, chatting up the head of the theater department for the university and hobnobbing with actors well into the next week. From then on it was nothing but theater crap—and I'd have to listen to her re-explain the whole thing to my parents when we got home. My consolation was, of course, the holy hours between ten and two. At two, Lizzy came home with Syl, and I usually had to hear her vague references to my "posing" and "panting" for the lovely Hungarian. Of course, I was usually still floating around the library at that time, so what did I care? I just had to ignore her ongoing acting cheer.

"It's so *perfectly* fabulous," she said. Again.

"You're so perfectly annoying," I muttered and flipped a page in my notebook. I'd been going through it pretty fast: notes on vampire lore, Zsòfia's eyes, the history of mythology, Zsòfia's skin, Vlad the Impaler, Zsòfia's ... other fine qualities.

"Oh, whatever. You didn't even pay attention to the play," she complained. "You were out there, scribbling in that thing."

"I was not—it was pitch dark," I lied and chewed on the pencil end. "What's a synonym for voluptuous?"

"Ugh. Don't make me gag!" Lizzy wretched.

"Luscious?"

"Gross! I'm glad you're going away on Saturday. I think you'd follow that girl to Mars."

"She's not from Mars. She's from Hungary," I corrected. But of course, Lizzy had just brought up the *other* thing destroying my happiness. Usually I think of my time with Aunt Syl as the longest two weeks of my life. Now, however, Saturday was looming like a thundercloud.

"Dinner is served!" sang my aunt as she leaned into the den. "Jake, you too—I have a little surprise for you."

"For—me?" I asked. This was new. She just bobbed her frizzy head and popped back into the hall.

"Maybe she wants to send a care package," Lizzy said, tossing a pillow at my stomach. "For your potty trouble."

"Oh shut up," I muttered and hopped over the back of the couch. The dining table was set—this time with three plates. *Not good*, I thought. But when I got close, I could see a white envelope on the platter.

"Um, thanks?" I said, picking it up and fingering the corner. Too light to be money....

"Open it! Open it!" Syl practically squealed—but then, with a serious effort, she put on a more somber face. "Oh, but perhaps you should sit down first, Jacob."

I tried really hard not to roll my eyes. And then I sat down. Inside the envelope was a pale blue card. It read:

You are invited!
What: Dinner at Dr. Sylvia's house
When: June 20, Friday night, 6pm
Why: To wish our guest a safe journey!
GUEST OF HONOR: JACOB MARESBETH

It was signed at the bottom by Syl herself, and Lizzy, and Leonard ... and *Zsòfia*.

Chapter 5

FRIDAY. I'VE ALWAYS LIKED FRIDAY; IT'S THE LAST DAY OF the week—no homework—and it's date night. For people who get dates. So far, I am not one of these. Or, well, not *technically*.

"So you have a date?? Holy crap, man!" said Henry over the phone. "When did you ask her out?"

"Oh. Well." I was holding the phone with my chin and shoulder, and balancing my notepad on one knee. "It's sort of a get-together thing. I mean, a couple people will be there. It's a dinner."

"Uh oh. You can't eat that stuff."

"S'alright." I switched ears. "I've got it covered. I'll tell her I'm into health food instead."

"Right, like juice bars and whatever?"—a pause, in which Henry made a mental note—"I bet *all* college chicks dig juice bars."

"I dunno. But she'll be here at six."

"Wow. Jake and the Grad Gal. Tony Peterson, eat your heart out!"

I appreciated the sentiment; Tony was the quarterback of the football team and mostly a jerk. But I bet *he* never went out with a graduate student. Not that I was going out with Zsòfia, of course. Or, not exactly.

"Hey, Jake!" my sister called up the stairs, and I hurried Henry off the phone.

"What?" I gulped, hopping to the door with one shoe on. "Are they here already?"

"Leonard is. He's *early*." Lizzy leaned against the stair-rail. "Wow. Did you comb your hair and everything?"

"Yeah. You should try it," I snapped, but it was a pointless jab. Lizzy's always wearing a ponytail. My own blond mop is a little less tidy as a rule.

"Well, since you're the *guest of honor* and all that, you should come down."

"Right, like Leonard's here for my sake," I rolled my eyes, but I was glad he came.

Of course, he was sort of a rival for Zsòfia—I'd figured that out the first day—but he was so clumsy, fidgety, and inept that he made me look pretty good. In fact, I sat next to him just to set off the contrast. Lizzy sat across from me, as though she was just waiting for me to make an idiot of myself—and Aunt Syl was patiently doing the death watch in case all the fuss gave me a "paroxysm." I didn't care; I was waiting for Zsòfia.

My aunt was still bustling about the kitchen when the doorbell rang—I swear to God I would have made it there first, but Leonard jumped at the same time and I tripped over him, so Lizzy got it.

"Hello! You are the actress!" Zsòfia said, shrugging off her pink shawl.

"Lizzy," Lizzy corrected. "Come on in, you've got *admirers*."

"Er, hi, Zsòfia," Leonard said, and he looked almost as mad at Lizzy as I did. His total lack of social skills gave me a minute to recover, though, and of course I'd been chatting Zsòfia up all week—

"I finished the book you lent me," I said, brushing him aside and handing Zsòfia *The History of the Carpathians*. "It's great."

"I am so glad you like it. Did you read the others, too?"

"Wow," Lizzy interrupted. "Do all research assistants get research assistants?" Zsòfia looked a little confused by the comment. I was fighting the urge to strangle my sister, but Syl saved the situation by announcing the first course.

Sylvia swept everyone to their chairs, and brought in a dinner salad and mixing tongs. I took my place and waited for it to register: it took about three seconds for Leonard and Zsòfia to realize that I had no plate. Not to worry, I thought; after all, I had been polishing up and rehearsing an explanation for just this moment—something polite and interesting that didn't make me sound like an invalid. I had just cleared my throat for delivery, but at that precise moment, my aunt returned with salad dressing and announced:

"Now, don't you worry about Jacob. His constitution is *much*, much too delicate for group dining! He *never* eats with the family, poor dear."

She winked and I swallowed. This wasn't too bad. The situation was not yet out of my control.

"Actually," I started, but then something happened which I wasn't expecting. I had just swept the table with a glance, and I noticed that Zsòfia was looking at me. *Looking*, looking. *At me*, at me.

"Never, Jacob?" she asked, peering at me with those deep, dark eyes. I had the rapt attention of a beautiful woman. Problem: I had forgotten how to talk. I moved my mouth around a little. Flopped my tongue a few times. Nothing happened. And, unfortunately for me, my aunt abhors a vacuum. As I wasn't up for the challenge, she was more than ready to bear my soul *for* me.

"*Never*," she confirmed dramatically. "Why, he's never had a mouthful in my presence; it's just tragic, really."

"Um," I managed.

"Just tragic," Lizzy added, bringing in the second course with a satanic grin. It was beef, and it was rare, and I hadn't had dinner yet. It wasn't fair.

"Yes, you wouldn't know it to look at him," Syl said, slicing into the stuff. "But he has a peculiar disease. Inscrutable!"

"Look," I stammered, "disease is kind of a strong word."

It was such a lame thing to say even I wouldn't have listened ... and before I knew it, we were up to our ears in the misleading medical jargon my aunt's been fed over the years. I *tried* to interrupt, really I did, but in the end all I could do was cross my fingers and hope neither constipation nor diarrhea entered the discussion.

"It's a rare form of the disorder epilepsy—thought to be related to 'falling sickness' in the late seventeenth and early eighteenth centuries," Syl chattered happily. "But the form it takes in Jacob is *truly* exceptional!"

"In a weird sort of way," Lizzy added.

"It makes him lethargic in the mornings and rather excitable at night, but there are a myriad of other *inscrutable* details. Do you know, it reminds me of hysteria! Really it does!" Aunt Syl congratulated herself for that, and everyone at the table gave me the I-am-sure-it-must-be-awful look. I could have died. Just imagine having your personal quirks laid bare in front of a live audience, delivered entirely in third person as if you weren't sitting *right there*.

"It must be very boring," Leonard said, clearly pleased with this turn of events. Zsòfia put her knife down.

"It is very odd, isn't it? What do you eat?" she asked.

I assumed this was directed at me, but I was once more saved from the trouble of talking about myself, this time by Lizzy.

"Oh, it's *really* dreadful," she said, shaking her head as if she possessed a hidden wealth of knowledge on the subject. There is such a thing as cool-factor; it's that "I know, but don't care to tell you" attitude that makes other people flock around your shrine. Some people have it, some don't, but Lizzy's got alarming amounts.

"And it *is* boring, actually. Looks just like paste and tastes like cardboard."

"Yes, dear Lizzy knows much more about it than I do," my aunt chimed in again. (That's right. Everybody knows more about Jake than Jake.) "But that isn't the worst of it, you know. He has perpetual anemia, requiring him to have blood transfusions all the time."

"Uh—Aunt Syl," I started, and across the table I saw Lizzy's face freeze up. "It's not really that important—"

"What is 'transfusions'? Could you explain to me?" Zsòfia asked, and now the melancholy squirrel seemed interested too.

"Does it happen at the hospital?" Leonard asked.

"No, it does *not*!" I said, a little more forceful than I meant to.

"No, no," my aunt corrected unhelpfully. "That's the very worst thing! He administers them *himself*...."

To be perfectly honest, I don't remember every word of what happened next. It's a defense mechanism, I guess. I stopped listening and started focusing all my attention on the blot of gravy on the tablecloth. It was about the shape of Wisconsin, I decided. A few more comments about my nervous habits passed over my head, and I even thought about faking a "paroxysm," just to end the episode. The whole dinner was an unqualified disaster, and I can't tell you how relieved I was when they finally arrived at dessert and coffee.

"... and, do you know, he brings a supply of blood with him just for the purpose," was my aunt's final remark as she finished her cheesecake. I was sliding lower in my chair, evaporating in the thin air of embarrassment. So, for a minute, I didn't hear Zsòfia said my name.

"Jacob?" she asked again. "Tell me, have you taken the blood since you have come?"

"I'm sorry, have I what?" I hadn't been following the conversation terribly closely.

"The blood—have you taken the blood these two weeks?" she asked. You might think this was an easy question to lie to, but I somehow tripped over the expression "taken the blood"; after all, these were supposed to be "transfusions." In any event, this linguistic hiccup caused me to hesitate. A lot. In silence. And at a table of English majors, such a lull in conversation is hard to miss. Unfortunately, before I could address the situation, Lizzy laid down her fork loudly and made a voluble "tsk" sound.

"What a highly impolite question," she said with profound disgust. My aunt and I were pretty shocked, but Zsòfia's look was harder to describe.

"Is it?" she asked with genuine surprise, "I am so very sorry, Jacob. I did not mean to insult you."

Now it was my turn to be disgusted. But not at her, of course.

"There is no reason to apologize, Zsòfia," I said. "It isn't any of Lizzy's business."

Lizzy's fork clattered again, this time out of real indignation; if looks were stakes, I'd be dead. My aunt's famed perception kicked in about then, and she decided to intervene by asking my sister to help with the dishes, leaving Leonard a little unsure of his next move.

"I—ah—thank you, Dr. Sylvia—" he coughed. "And Jacob. So nice—all of it. I should—it's late."

"Certainly, certainly! I don't mean to keep my young scholars from their efforts!" Syl called as she carried the stacked plates into the adjoining room. Leonard gave me a look that was hard to describe; not dislike, exactly. More like distaste. Honestly, though, he looked far more prone to nervous fits than I ever did.

"Goodbye, Zsòfia," he said, and then excused himself to do some nice, safe research at the library. I wasn't sorry to see him go … but that still left three of us at the table. Me, Zsòfia and my wounded pride. Interestingly, the complete obliteration of self-respect made me more or less at ease. After all, what could I possibly say to make myself look worse than my aunt had? I pushed the mostly untouched coffee away and smiled weakly.

"Some going-away dinner, eh?"

I was expecting her to laugh a little, to humor the kid with the crush, and to say something nice about my personality. But she didn't do any of those things. She did something else entirely. She leaned forward and kissed me on the forehead.

"I—ooh," I said, sounding more breathy and light-headed than I'd like to admit.

"I am glad you were not offended," she said.

My brain had become a complete blank. It was as if Zsòfia's graduate-student personality had just stepped aside to reveal something or someone else. It's like that girl that you see every day in class with the same uniform, the same glasses, and the same hair-do, only this time you see her at the beach in a bikini. Same person, but *not the same*. And this new Zsòfia leaned forward with an earnest expression and said,

"I do not wish you to go away."

"You're kidding," I said. Smooth, I know, but I actually thought I was hallucinating.

"I was only getting to know you." She shrugged her pretty (bare) shoulders. "It is a shame that you cannot stay like your sister."

Now, my brain had undergone a bit of a shock, but it had just gone from full-stop to full-tilt. *Could I stay?* Dad wouldn't leave until the next morning.... If I called right now, I could get permission. But I could hear my mother's voice in my head: *You know he overeats when he's depressed.*

"Well, perhaps I could stay a bit longer," I muttered dreamily (while mentally counting the number of blood bags still in my cooler.) Why had I been so wasteful? I'd consumed two thirds or more of what I'd brought! Then again, I really didn't need to eat *every* day, right? I could ration. I could make it.

"I would be very pleased," Zsòfia said, and she touched my hand. Feather soft—and I made an embarrassing chirping sound.

"*Chirrup*—I mean, sure. Sure, that would be great."

A quick call to my dad, a quick explanation to my aunt, and, well, you get the picture. I was reveling in Zsòfia's sudden warmth when my sister returned for the coffee cups, and I continued to be fuzzy and happy even after Zsòfia left for home.

Unfortunately, my new idea encountered more resistance than I thought it would.

"Jacob Alexander Maresbeth!" my mother snapped. I was actually talking to my dad, but I could hear her half-shouting over his shoulder.

"Seriously, Dad. I just haven't been that hungry. You know. We've been, ah, busy and everything."

The tricky part about the situation was this: I'm a lousy liar. It seems inconsistent, I'm sure, since I'm always telling some story or other to account for my condition. But those are lies I've grown up with and they've come to be second nature; sometimes I half believe them myself. This was entirely different. This was lying *to my parents*, which is something only Lizzy can do with any proficiency.

"Jake, two weeks is a long time."

"I know, but Mom made me take a bunch extra—you know she did," I said, crossing my fingers. There was a pause as he related this to my mother. Then there was a scuffling sound as Mom wrestled the cell phone away from him.

"Jake, you tell me *exactly* how many are left. I'm serious."

"Twenty," I lied.

"Are you lying, Jake?"

"Mom! Dad packed 42, you added six more to the top compartment on my way out the door—how could I possibly get through all that?" Technically, this was *not* a lie. It was just logic sliced very thin.

"Twenty for almost fourteen days? That's not even two for each day. You're sure?"

"Positive." O-positive, actually. I heard the phone being handed back to Dad for the final OK. Turns out, he was easier. He was the one who had to drive up from Virginia to get me, after all. So within an hour after the dinner party, I was safely reinstalled as house guest for another two weeks—two blissful weeks pouring over gothic tales of horror with a dark-eyed, fair-skinned sylph. I was in for happy dreams, I can tell you.

Or would have been, had Lizzy been content to let me get some sleep. I walked upstairs, flipped on the light, and came face to face with one angry fourteen-and-a-half-year-old.

"I'd like to know what you think you're doing," she demanded.

"And I'd like to know what you're doing in my *room*. Come on, out—I wanna get some sleep."

"You're nocturnal, you twit. And I *won't* get out," she said.

"Fine," I walked past her and pulled her ponytail. "You can watch me sleep."

"Before your *dinner?*" she asked, raising her eyebrows.

"Ate earlier."

"You suck at lying," she hissed. "Of course, you suck a lot of things. Vampire."

"Beat it." I flopped on my stomach and put a pillow over my head. That would have been a signal to most people that the conversation was over, but not for Lizzy. And there's nothing like having ninety-eight pounds come crashing into the small of your back. I'd been in a good mood, but I don't appreciate being tackled. I stood straight up, even with all her weight, and knocked her onto the floor.

"What is wrong with you?" I demanded. She was on her feet again and scowling.

"Me? *Nothing* is wrong with *me*. You, on the other hand, have some explaining to do. I heard what you told Mom over the phone—not hungry! Ha! You've been sucking those things down like there's no tomorrow. How much *do* you have left?"

"Geez, Liz, get a grip. I know how much I have, and I know how much I need."

"Which isn't to say that you *have* as much as you *need*," she snapped. She's a quick one, my sister. "You are just doing this to hang out with Helga the Hungarian!"

"*Zsòfia*—are you not able to pronounce it or something? And so what? Why do you care who I hang out with? You'll be at camp the whole time."

"Yeah, I know. That's the whole problem!" she said. Which I thought was odd.

"I don't believe it!" I laughed. "You're actually jealous! I mean really, I'm touched and all, but it's a little immature of you."

This was not a very kind thing to say, perhaps. And probably not very smart, either. Lizzy turned several shades of I-don't-know-what, and came at me with all ten fingernails. (This is her favorite attack position.) I caught her in mid-flight.

"That's it!" I shouted, picking her right up off the floor and tossing her into the hallway. She looked ridiculous, sitting on her butt out there, but I shut the door before laughing my head off. Victory at last! Peace on earth!

But alas, no sleep. Whether it was the result of my excitement for the next day (when Zsòfia would make her Saturday visit and Lizzy would be safely interred at camp), or the energy I'd built up in expelling my sister from the room, I couldn't close my eyes for hours. Instead, I ended up dosing off sometime in the wee hours of morning.

Chapter 6

MY SISTER IS RIGHT; I AM NOCTURNAL BY NATURE. She thinks it's a vampire thing. I think it's a *me* thing. I don't even like the way the world *smells* before 10 am. Give me the graveyard shift, thank you. But of course, the longer you stay awake at night, the harder it is to get up in the morning. So, I wasted half a precious Saturday looking at the back of my lids, and when I finally opened them, my alarm clock announced that it was right around noon.

"Crap!"

That would be panic. But panic is bad, especially to a groggy head and an empty stomach. I'd managed to get one foot on the floor, but the other one was wrapped up in sheets like a sailors' knot ... and in trying to get out of bed I fell flat on my face. My chin connected with plank flooring and for a minute, I thought I should just stay there. But of course, Zsòfia arrived at noon—as in, immediately. I shoved myself up and slithered out of the sheets and into my bathroom, but halfway between tooth-brushing and showering my aunt poked her head into my room.

"Jacob, dear?"

"Ga—Aunt Syl!" I nearly choked on the toothpaste—which is definitely *not* part of my diet.

"Zsòfia's in the study," she began, totally clueless to the fact that I was in my boxers and not really up for company just yet. "I'm just popping out to do a bit of shopping, but won't you offer her some lunch? There's a good boy! Leftovers are in the blue tins and fresh cheese in the white—fruit on the side board—oh, and did you see the special soap?"

"Ah. Soap?"

"Of course, dear—it's medicated!" she said, winking at my apparent stupidity and then bobbing out of sight again. I stood there chewing my toothbrush and staring at nothing. Did she want me to make Zsòfia's lunch? That was almost the weirdest thing anyone had ever asked me to do; I don't even know what most food is for, much less how to assemble it. Then again, there was something sort of thrilling about the idea.... Make Zsòfia lunch. Zsòfia. Who was already downstairs and waiting.

"I'll be right down!" I called. I shut off the shower, tried to splash my face with water, get a comb through my longish hair, and get dressed all at the same time. Considering my handicapped morning motor skills, I think I managed pretty well. But, alas, I was not exactly putting my best foot forward. Zsòfia greeted me at the bottom of the stairs ... and pointed out that my shirt was inside out.

"So it is," I said, looking down. I was actually trying to think of some plausible reason for it to *be* inside out.

"Are you feeling quite well?" she asked in her lilting accent.

"Um, sure?"

"Good, good." She turned her back on me, then, and headed for the library. This was perfectly normal, of course. Normal as in last-night-never-happened normal.

"Ah, are you feeling—fine too?" I asked. So lame. It's just embarrassing.

"Mmmm," Zsòfia nodded, unpacking her bag and settling in. Professional courtesy. Polite conversation. Absolutely no hint of anything else. I was actually paralyzed by this, somehow, and I ended up standing on the stairs for a full five minutes. Dreams were evaporating—I'd imagined the whole thing.

My own book (a copy of German vampire lore) was on the coffee table. I went to get it and took the moment to invert my shirt before I returned to the library. Okay. So I'd been wrong. I *still* got to spend two more weeks talking literature and film with the most beautiful woman on earth ... and it's not like I was going to do any less bragging to Henry.

"This one has a timeline," I said, sitting across from her and flipping to the index. Zsòfia looked up, a smile-crease forming around her pretty lips.

"You are very studious. I will look. And you can see here—I bring the pictures of Budapest."

She handed me a book of historical photos, and I confess, I actually was interested enough to forget to stare at Zsòfia. I also forgot what my aunt had said about lunch. That is, until my own stomach started making a fuss. I'd skipped dinner the night before, after all.

"Oh, hey," I said, putting the book down. "Aunt Syl thought you might like some lunch? I could, ah, make it for you. If you want."

It's funny. That sounded just as strange coming from me as it had from Syl. Would she want me to make her lunch? Is that like a date? Do people do lunch dates? I started to sweat, which was not sexy (especially since I'd skipped the shower)—but Zsòfia put down her pen and smiled.

"You would make lunch for me? That is very sweet."

"Sure! I'll just—go get it," I hopped up, but she waved her hand.

"Thank you, I brought my own today, Jacob. But you will eat?"

I hesitated.

"I already did. You know. Upstairs."

"Your special food," Zsòfia nodded sympathetically. "Your aunt tells me."

"Right," I sat back down, feeling a little gripe in my mid-section. Special food all right. And rare, too, at that moment. Zsòfia produced her own little meal from a metal tiffin tin, and I went back to pretending not to stare at her. It wasn't a thrilling love story, I'm sure you'll agree, but the rest of the afternoon went by pretty smoothly all the same—five glorious hours. Five vamp-filled, studiously gothic hours of which I remembered nothing except that Zsòfia brushed my hand once while reaching for a notecard—and before I knew it, my aunt's car was crunching up the driveway again.

"There you are, such studious scholars!" she tweeted, sweeping into the room in several colors of skirt, none of which matched. "Why, it's nearly five!"

"I must be going, then," Zsòfia said, puckering her forehead and looking at her watch.

"You won't stay for dinner, my dear?" Aunt Syl asked out loud (and I begged inside my own head). Zsòfia shook her head, which, I should add, sent waves of that golden hair cascading over her shoulders. Then, she smiled at me, thanked me for the use of my book, and walked in that marvelous way of hers to the door. I watched her the whole way, trying to feed off every last little minute.

"So, Jacob dear, what do you make of Zsòfia?" my aunt said while twirling the end of her scarf. I blanked. It wasn't that I couldn't think of plenty to say, it's just that lots of it had to do with some part of her anatomy.

"Oh, well, you know," I said, stalling.

"Yes, her research is going well, I think—though she has much to do before she can begin the dissertation in earnest."

Research. Right. I had no idea what we were talking about, but I thought it would be safe to nod and act agreeable. Nodding is a good tactic with my aunt. It gives her the impression you are encouraging her to carry the conversation herself, and that usually eliminates the need for adding your own independent thoughts. True to form, she went on a while in that vein, talking about who knows what in the weird science of getting a PhD. You might think I'd be annoyed, but I wasn't. I'd had almost no sleep and was due for a meal. I guess I was riding on lovesick adrenaline while

Zsòfia was there, but I'd just hit a solid brick wall of exhaustion and wanted to go upstairs and die. Syl might have been talking to the cats; I didn't care.

"... Well, *cést la vie*. Tell me dear, would you like to join me for dinner? Simply as a congenial table companion—I wouldn't ask you to tax yourself."

"Oh, um—you know, I'm really tagged out," I said, forgetting that my aunt would have no idea that was slang for "I'm tired, please leave me alone."

"Capital! We'll sit in the kitchen; it's just the two of us," she said brightly. I was about to protest, but she'd bustled off already. And at this moment, I suddenly missed my sister a great deal. First, she usually translated between Aunt Syl and me, and second, when she was around, my presence was never really that necessary. They chatted about theater and English and who knows what kind of girl stuff and basically let me be (my aunt is terribly uninterested in journalism or wind surfing). Now I was the stand-in, however, and in my sleep-walking state, I wasn't going to be very "congenial" at all.

"There you are, a nice cup of tea," my aunt said when we were settled at the little kitchen table. I didn't want any tea. But there you go.

"I wonder how your sister is finding camp? She's so very talented, you know. *Naturalement!*" she said. (I think its French and probably a compliment.)

"However," she continued, spearing a carrot, "I was concerned that you might be lonely without her."

"It's fine—I mean, I'm fine. Lots to do," I yawned. I was feeling a little foggy-headed, and even though the sun was setting, I didn't feel much more alert.

"Yes, the museums are brilliant, aren't they?" Syl said, as though we'd been talking about them. "Incidentally, if you have time, there is a fantastic display of stained glass in the Cemetery Chapel. I sent Zsòfia there just the other day. She's enamored with such places, but then, she has rather peculiar hobbies."

"I think she's great," I said, roused a bit at the possibility of defending her. Yes, my delusions had gotten that far already.

"I agree—an excellent student and a worthy young lady. It's truly generous of her to spend a little of her time with you. Knowing your delicate nature, she was undoubtedly vexed at the effect your sister's absence might have on your constitution."

My aunt delivered this with a totally unconcerned air, totally ignorant that in my head her words translated into "Die, ego! Die! Die!" My heart bottomed out somewhere near my Achilles tendon.

"You know," I said after a moment's recovery, "I think I'll turn in."

"Aren't you feeling well, my dear?"

"No—I mean, yes, I'm great. I just want to be rested for church," I said, which was a great save because there was a lot of truth in it.

My aunt, one of those annoying morning people, goes to a church service that begins at seven-thirty. Seven-thirty *in the morning*! We don't even know if God gets *up* that early. What if he'd like to have some coffee and set the universe in order before being addressed by a billion churchgoers? Anyhow, that answer seemed sufficient so I was released from the ego-bashing and made my way upstairs.

When I got to my room, I pulled the cooler out from under the bed and took a look at the contents. It was looking sort of sparse in there. I was hungry—but I was actually too tired to be *really* hungry, so I decided to go one more day. I'd done that before once, in a pinch, but three days was definitely my limit. I deliberated a bit more, then shut the lid and slid the thing back under my bed. I think my next intended action was to undress, but even though it was only seven in the evening, I fell asleep before I got to it.

The buzzer sounded at six-thirty. I'd been sleeping for almost twelve hours by then ... but it didn't really improve things. I got up. I just didn't open my eyes, which meant I nearly broke my neck getting into the shower. I sort of slouched against the cold tile for a while, trying to remember how to use soap. Hot water was a bust, so I tried switching to cold. This had some unfriendly consequences that I won't share, but it did *not* help wake me up. In fact, I only managed a half-open squint while choosing my clothes, and once dressed, I slumped onto the edge of my bed and put my face in my hands. I was totally miserable—weak and about half sick.

It actually took me a full fifteen minutes of consciousness before I realized what the problem was. I was *hungry*. I decided that I'd have to eat something if I was going to be awake for the sermon, but before I had a chance to take care of that, my aunt tripped into the room and hustled me out the door. We were late, I guess, and that pretty much absorbed her attention (otherwise she might have noticed that I slept through the sermon). I only really woke up when we got back to the car, and apparently the wear and tear was starting to show.

"Jacob, my dear," Syl tilted her head, then reached over and tilted mine. "You look rather unwell, I think?"

"I'm pretty tired," I admitted.

"Bless you! Why didn't you *say* so! I'll take you straight home and then up you go for a nap, young man!"

And for once, I didn't argue.

But it just wasn't meant to be. My stomach gripe had turned into a full-out bellow, but I'd promised myself to wait until dinner. Unfortunately, my will power was breaking down. If I went to my room, I'd definitely throw back a pint. Chances were good I'd do another by dinner. Then where would I be? In trouble with Mom and Dad, that's for certain. So, once we got back to Syl's place, I put on a happy face and said I "needed some air."

This ruffled feathers. I'm lucky I got away from the house without a parasol and a wheelchair. But I *did* manage to squeak away, winding my way through the tree-lined neighborhood on autopilot. By four, I was ready to flag down the bloodmobile, so I sat on the porch. Around six I started to crack. It was sunset *somewhere*, I reasoned, and so I ducked into the house and charged up the stairs without saying hi to my aunt. I actually swung the cooler onto my bed, grabbed the topmost bag, and I put it down so fast I got hiccups. For a minute, I just enjoyed the not-starving sensation, then I dropped the empty container into the cooler and started zipping the flap.

That's when I heard it. A soft step behind me. In my hurry, I had not only forgotten to lock the door, I'd forgotten to close it! But the person behind me wasn't my aunt.

It was Zsòfia.

"Uh—I didn't know you were, um," I muttered, trying to hide the big (and blazingly blue) cooler behind me.

"I am sorry, did I interrupt you?" she asked, "The door was open and your aunt told me you had come upstairs."

This was unfair; I had to process too many things at once:

How do I not be an idiot?

Why did my aunt send her up to my bedroom—

She's in my bedroom.

She's in my bedroom.

"Um, no, you weren't interrupting. I was—er—just checking my cooler," I said.

She looked intently at the zippered cooler on the bed.

"This is of the blood?" she asked. Now *I* felt like the twitch doing the wave. She had a funny way of talking sometimes, and I stumbled all over the answer.

"Yeah—for it, that is. It has to be a certain temperature and all. I was checking it," I said.

Zsòfia nodded slowly and gave me a look of deep concern, but it was a far cry from my aunt's "poor dear" look. This was sympathetic, sexy concern ... this was night-of-the-dinner-party concern.

"How frustrating it must be to think of it all the time," she said, reaching forward to touch my face.

"Ye-yeah," I said, feeling the warm, fuzzy tingle running up my spine.

"How do you know when you need one?" she asked.

"Er?" Warm fuzzy interrupted.

"A transfusion—how do you know?"

"I can just tell. It's internal," I said, which, technically, is true. She released my chin, and for the second time, I witnessed the not-graduate-student Zsòfia. Transformation was taking place right in front of me. And it was hot.

"Are you well, Jacob?" she asked, which was the same question she'd asked in the morning ... but not at all in the same way. I felt a little dizzy, and I know I was making this stupid half-grin....

"Sometimes," I said dreamily. She smiled reached into her bag.

"I am so glad," she said, then handed me a little dark-colored book. "I stopped by only quickly; I forgot to give this to you."

"Oh, thanks very much," I said, but my confusion must have been showing.

"You do not know this book?" she asked. I shook my head.

"Should I?"

"I only thought you might have heard of it—you can keep it for tonight," She shrugged her shoulders lightly. "I will come for it tomorrow."

She was backing away. I didn't want her to leave, but how do you ask someone to stay longer in your bedroom without it sounding, well, exactly like that? I didn't want to appear desperate or carnal—or desperately carnal. So I wished her goodnight instead, and she rustled down the stairs and out of the front door.

Just like the Friday before, it took me a minute to reconnect to reality. I was reveling in the rebirth of my ego after all. Given that, and the fuzzy-headed feeling, it was a full twenty minutes before I bothered to look at the book.

What can I say? It was an evening of surprises.

Inscribed on the front cover were the words: *A Vampire's Bible.*

Chapter 7

Vampire. Bible.
I stared a minute, and then I dodged back to the bed and tucked it under the comforter. It wasn't the sort of book I wanted Aunt Syl to see me reading (I mean, *really*), and it was a little early to hit the sack. I went downstairs instead, but of course Zsòfia had already gone.

"Uh, Aunt Syl?" I asked, poking my head into the TV room. She was apparently watching the news and reading the paper at the same time—while balancing a cup of tea and a sandwich on her left knee.

"There you are!" she piped. "Did Zsòfia find you?"

"Er, yeah—"

"And she gave you the book, then?"

"The book?" I chirped. I couldn't help it. "You know about *The Vam—*"

"Know about it! You silly thing, I *gave* it to her. I knew you would enjoy it, too!" Aunt Syl tried to bob her head enthusiastically, but almost upset her teacup. "After all, you've always enjoyed *architecture*!"

And for a minute, I just stared at her. For one thing, I've never given a second thought to architecture ... and for another, *The Vampire Bible* was clearly *not* about building plans.

"You gave her—a book—to give to me?" I asked, trying to put it all together in some sensible way.

"Not at all! Or, well, yes, rather," she said, smiling as though that was clarifying. "She is fascinated by history, you know, and I lent her my copy of *Cleveland's Historic Buildings*. Only yesterday I was telling her how much you enjoyed such things—and so she was kind enough to pop over with it. Thoughtful young lady!"

I think I managed some vague response to this, but my brain was having a conniption. Zsòfia had lied to my aunt—why would she do that? What was in that book, anyway? Maybe there was a note of some sort in there?

"Bedtime!" I said, backing out of the sitting room at top speed. My heart had just hit full gallop. *What was in the book??* I bounced up the stairs, three steps at a time and scattered the cats on the landing. *A note?* Or, better yet, *a photo???* I rushed into my room and bolted the door. No need for unexpected guests. I dug the book out and flopped onto the pillows.

The cover was warped a little, and the pages stuck together in a gross kind of way, but the front flap did not contain a loving inscription. It did have writing on it though, in watery-looking ink: *1835*. The date, I guessed, which would explain its antique condition. I flipped to the front cover, which was brittle and yellowish. The title was there again, but no author. Instead, there was a quote—and I recognized it. It shows up in *Dracula*, too, and it supposed to be from some old poem: *"for the dead travel fast."*

"Comforting," I muttered, but I kept turning pages, hoping to see a little hand-written note somewhere, or maybe—you know—a phone number. Instead, I got the confidential memo of some wacko. It was creepy—not in the horror-story kind of way, but in the you-have-a-stalker kind of way. Written in *first person*, it went something like this:

> Tell me, friend, have you grown tired of their prying eyes? Are you not weary of pretending to be what you are not? I know the long hours you have spent, waiting, watchful, worried that your closest associates might turn you out of doors. They don't understand you. How could they? But I understand you. Perfectly.

I felt my skin prickle. And it got weirder. I opened my note pad and started scribbling notes.

> Do not fear. You aren't alone, after all, and those who know you will also protect you. It is our duty and our solemn privilege, my brothers and sisters. And so, I put forth this script as a record of lessons learned, as a guide for the young and as a warning against those of the world who would hunt and destroy what they cannot possibly understand.

I swallowed a little thickly and put the pencil down. In my head, the author had Bela Lugosi's accent—and while the word "vampire" never showed up anywhere else except the title, it was all over every page: *sufferer, stranger, monster, master*. The sun was just going down, and though I am usually hip to the night scene, I was actually sorry to see it go. I turned on both reading lamps and the overhead, all while continuing to read the book. It was too weird to leave alone, much weirder than fiction. Mostly because it didn't seem to be fiction at all. Two-hundred and seventy pages of—well—advice. It was like a conduct manual for psychopaths, with lots of recommendations about feeding the "animal nature." And it ended with an invitation: *seek out your own.*

"Not a chance in Hades," I thought, shaking my head and flipping to the very back. I probably should have started at the end, because that's when I found what I'd been looking for—Zsòfia's handwriting. On the last page, which was blank, she'd written something in pencil. It wasn't a love note. It wasn't for me at all, though it might as well have been. At least, I almost jumped out of my skin when I saw it: *Grindelwald, Switzerland.*

I should explain that. See, I was just convincing myself that this was a coded text of some underground revolution or other. Or that maybe it was a realistic piece of fiction. But then: there was Switzerland. I shut the book and chewed my thumb for a minute. I've been there, see. *Grindelwald.* I was eight, and it was the last family vacation we took before I developed my, er, digestion issues. Eighteen feet of snow, picture-perfect ski resort—doesn't exactly jive with Count D, does it? But that's where I got ill, and that's where the book was from, and suddenly I felt the tiniest bit worried. What if this wasn't fiction ... and what if this isn't epilemia? I shook my head. It's dumb to think that way, and my dad would be seriously disappointed in my lack of scientific whatever.... But I was still mulling it over when I fell asleep, and still thinking about it when I woke up, too. And let's face it, nagging question number one was this: Why did Zsòfia give the book to *me?*

Since I'd finally eaten something the previous night, my morning went much better. The sun was shining and it was almost like actual summer. I'd missed Aunt Syl, who was off early to teach her summer class, but she'd left out the nasty tea substitute just in case I needed "cleansing." I didn't. So instead, I walked around the house in circles, tapping the book against my jeans and waiting for Zsòfia to get there. I'd been rehearsing a speech about the Vamp Bible, since I didn't want to seem ungrateful, but I also wanted to know why she gave it to me, and why she *didn't* tell Aunt Syl. Smart and sophisticated, but not whiney or accusing—that's what I was aiming for. Not that it mattered much.

I saw Zsòfia before she saw me—through the screen door. The sun was shining slick on her hair, as she leaned her bike against the porch. Now, I'm not particularly fashion conscious, but I won't ever forget the dress. It was white. And it sort of clung to things in a way I appreciated.

"Here is your book," I said, meeting her at the door.

"Oh yes—I need it for my work," she said, sticking it in her bag and walking through to the library. I followed in her wake.

"It's pretty ... old," I added.

"Oh, yes. The nineteenth century. I found it in a book store in Edinburgh." She set her bag on the floor of the library like she always did, and opened her notebook like she always did. There was absolutely nothing suspicious about anything she did—unless you count the fact that she seemed almost totally uninterested in me being there at all. Again.

"Oh?" I said. "Edinburgh and not—not Switzerland?"

Zsòfia leaned her chin on her hand and blinked at me.

"No. You have been to Switzerland?" she asked.

"Ski trip," I said, and tried to think of how Lizzy would play it off. "The place is full of rich watch-makers, you know?"

"I think it is very interesting," she added, plucking a pencil from behind her ear.

"The book? I guess," I said. "But Aunt Syl said you had a book for me on—er, architecture."

"Yes, I left it for you on the coffee table."

I stopped and stared over her shoulder. So she had. Right there, face up, with my name written on a post-it note was a slender, sepia-toned paperback. I never even noticed it.

"Oh." My brain ground gears again. "But *The Vampire Bible*? You just wanted to, ah, share it…?"

"You do not like it? Ah well!" She plucked it from my fingers cheerfully. "It will go in my dissertation, chapter two."

And, with a pretty shake of her head, that was that. The subject simply dropped through this black hole or something; she had shifted her attention to a set of gothic short fiction stories and was asking what I knew about Polish folklore.

You can't imagine how stupid I suddenly felt. It's like having a nightmare that terrifies you, but then when you go to tell someone else about it, it's the dumbest thing you've ever heard yourself say. I crossed the room to my chair, picked up my notebook, and crossed out several very stupid sentences about where this was all going. Some investigative journalist. I picked up the architecture book instead, though I didn't look at it. I just used it as a screen to sneak looks at Zsòfia. That sounds stupid and childish, I know—but I was *hoping* to catch her sneaking looks at *me*.

The sun was hot coming through the window; I guessed it to be after five o'clock—meaning I'd spent four and a half hours watching Zsòfia not look at me. I slumped in my seat and put the book down; Syl would be there before too long, and another day of not getting anywhere would have passed me by. Zsòfia was engrossed, busy scribbling notes in the long shadow from the bookcase. *The Vampire Bible* was out on the table again—and it was sitting in a pool of yellow-red light, which made it look a little sickly.

"So, what's chapter two about?" I asked. I don't know what made me do it; I had determined to distance myself from it, and here I was, bringing it back up again.

Zsòfia raised her eyes and looked at me through her brows.

"Do you mean the chapter I write on this?" she asked, tapping the book.

"Yeah. *The Vamp Bible.*" Sad. I was like a moth to a flame.

"Sexual politics," she said.

"You—ah—really?" I coughed, realizing my voice had taken on a slightly chirpy quality. Zsòfia blinked in the late afternoon light and looked at her watch.

"It is late, Jacob! You should not let me stay so long," and then, with a graceful sweep, she pushed all her work into the waiting bag. My heart skipped—it always seemed to when I realized she was leaving, but as the word "sexual" was still floating around in my brain it was practically sprinting.

"You said—um, politics?" I asked, walking her to the front door. Or, well, following her there like a lost puppy. She stopped short at the screen door and I almost bumped into her. The sensation caused my brain to seize up and I stuttered to a halt, looking stupefied. Zsòfia gave me a quizzical look.

"Are you embarrassed to talk to me?" she asked, tilting her head.

"Well, yeah, sometimes," I said helplessly. So uncool it's painful.

"Really?" she smiled. "You know you do not have to be. Not with me, Jacob. And yes. Sexuality is very much a part of my work. Did you not feel the passion of *The Vampire Bible*?"

"Ah—well—not really," I admitted, though I was feeling something, that's for sure. The sun was low and red, and Zsòfia's face was inches from mine.

"It is there, all the same," she said—and suddenly, she leaned forward, just a little. I panicked: *Was this a kiss moment? Was I supposed to kiss her—now—on those amazing lips??* I froze like an idiot, and then, before I made my next move, the screen door was banging closed behind her. She was gone, pushing her bicycle down the street and waving to my aunt, who was just coming up the drive.

Me? I stood there staring until my aunt came up the steps.

"Why, Jacob! Were you waiting for me?" She patted my head like I was a well-behaved dog and then handed me one of her many oversized bags. "Was Zsòfia here today? How odd!"

"It is?"

"Well, certainly!" she blinked and puckered her mouth up like a button. "Leonard was expecting her all afternoon; they were meeting for lunch. How strange—she's usually so good about ... Jacob, are you quite all right??"

She asked because I was grinning like an idiot. Really. I caught my reflection in the hall mirror and it was a cross between sugar-high and psychopath.

"I'm great," I chirped. *Zsòfia had skipped out on Leonard....* I could hardly believe it. She had been so distant, at least I thought so, but suddenly a fuzzy picture was starting to come into focus. Was the vampire book just an excuse to see me? Was the nerdy scholar thing just a mask to hide her increasing desire? And if that *was* a kiss moment—would there be more? I could have done back flips.

"Great!" I said again, "great" being the only word left in my vocabulary, then I turned my back on Syl before she could invite me to join her for tea. I went upstairs instead—to revel.

There was only one problem. If she was interested, how on earth was I supposed to keep her that way? This called for backup. And I really only had one go-to person.

"Henry, I gotta talk to you," I practically shouted into the cell phone.

"Can I call you after dinner?"

"No! Listen—I need advice."

There was a pause. Henry is not the person you normally go to for advice, and he knows it. This was just proof I was serious.

"What's up, Jake?"

"I think she digs me."

"The graduate chick? Awesome! So—what's the problem?"

This was a good question. The problem was I had no idea how to woo a 24-year-old Hungarian Venus. My best effort so far had been to make mostly inane comments about Bela Lugosi films.

"Well, what now? *You've* dated"—painful to admit—"do I ask her out? Do I buy flowers? What?"

"I thought you'd been out already!"

"No—yes—sort of. Look, she's hot and amazing and smart. I've pretty much exhausted everything I can think of to tell her. Give me something, Henry!"

"I don't even know her!" Henry protested, and I thumped my fist against my forehead. *Think—think—*

"She likes old, weird books. She likes black-and-white films. She's into Bela Lugosi and vampires—"

"Well, there you go!"

"There I go *what*, Henry?"

"You're a vampire! She should totally dig that!"

I almost choked.

"I can't tell her about that stuff!" I insisted, standing up again. "My dad would kill me! You know it's epilemia or whatever."

"Hey, you drink blood, right? And she likes vampires. You're practically a gold mine of weirdness!" Henry seemed very pleased with himself.

"Gee, thanks," I muttered. But I have to admit, he had a point. Let's face it, I was sitting on a piece of pretty incredible news for the gothic historian. Real Live Vampire!! Feel free to examine more closely! I didn't say a word of this to Henry, of course. But the temptation was *right there*, and the angst was tearing me up.

Actually, my stomach was also tearing me up, and it was only Monday. I had to wait until Wednesday, the third day of my enforced fast. And frankly, I wasn't sure I would make it. I'd made a little chart in my notepad, trying to figure up exact sums to keep me on my feet until the weekend ... but it was much worse than the first three-day fast. Apparently it was not cool to do this twice in a row.

By the time Wednesday dawned, my legs felt like a couple of sandbags. It would be fine for just hanging around Syl's library with Zsòfia, but unfortunately my goddess was helping out at the summer school till Thursday. I didn't even have a reasonable distraction from my grumbling stomach. It was enough to make me start questioning my resolve, I can tell you. If I kept it up much longer, I wouldn't need to worry about whether to tell Zsòfia about my condition or not ... I'd be mentally comatose.

"Do you want anything, Jacob?" Aunt Syl was doing her thing in the kitchen, making microwaved health food and talking to Byron and Shelley in conversational French.

"S'alright," I called from the landing. I'd been avoiding her a little. I felt crappy and didn't really want to give her more reasons to nurse-stalk me. Anyhow, I wouldn't be able to hear her over my stomach anyhow ... so by five after five I was digging under my bed for the cooler strap.

Trouble was, I couldn't reach it.

Bigger trouble was, it wasn't there.

Hunh? I grimaced. This did not make sense. I tried deep breathing and thinking it through. Did I move it? No. Did Aunt Syl move it? *Maybe.* I scrambled down stairs with this half-formed thought and slid (socks, slippery tile) right into her back.

"Ooo!" she chirped and pitched a head of lettuce on the floor. "Goodness, Jacob!"

"Sorry—Aunt Syl, did you move my cooler?"

"You're cooler?"

"Cooler. Blue. Plugs in. Has wheels. *Did you move it?*"

"No, dear, I haven't been in your room," she started, but then turned suddenly to scrutinize my face. "What is the matter, my dear? You look—"

"Panicked! Yes! It's not there!" I panted. "I mean, it was there before, and now it's *not!*" (which was really saying the same thing, but I was distraught).

"Are you sure you didn't move it?" she asked. I shook my head so hard I thought it might come off.

"No, I didn't move it!!" I managed to say that without unclenching my teeth, but then I got a grip and tried a more pragmatic approach. "If I moved it, then I would know where it was."

"Maybe you moved it and simply don't remember," she offered and my head nearly exploded.

"Ididn'tmovethecooler!! SOMEONE has TAKEN it!!" And then I started looking around as if I expected the robbers to still be in the house somewhere.

"Oh, Jake," Aunt Syl was speaking very gently. "Who would steal a cooler?"

"I—um, it—well," was all I managed to say.

She petted my arm.

"Perhaps you had better have another look upstairs. I'm sure it is there somewhere."

"Aunt Syl," I said, but I didn't follow it with anything because right about then reality started leaking back into my head, and I began to see the total implausibility of it. A thief snuck into the house, passed by my aunt's art pieces, television, stereo, and furniture to steal a cooler from an upstairs bedroom?

"I'll look," I grumbled, and returned to my room. I wasn't really intending to search for it, but I had nothing else to do and wasn't sure of my next move, so I kicked open the closet door and started shoving through the dirty clothes on the floor. Much to my surprise, something blue caught my eye at the far corner of my bed. Just at the wall where the window curtain hung down, I saw the strap. My heart just about jumped through my throat—but in a good way. The stupid thing had been there all along, but had been shoved so far under the bed that it was hidden by the curtain on the other side. After a nice deep breath, I grabbed the strap and swung the cooler onto the bed....

But something *else* was wrong. It was too light. My heart, which I'd been chewing on a minute before, dropped right through my spleen as I opened the zipper. I'd found the bag, but all the containers inside it were empty.

"What is going *on* here?" I said to nobody. After all, this was even weirder than before. Who in their right mind would steal blood? Is there a rogue Red Cross? My mind was spinning and I didn't dare try this one on my aunt, so I picked up my phone and called home.

It was not a pleasant conversation.

"What do you mean, *just the blood is gone?*" My father asked.

"All the containers are empty, Dad! Somebody just—I don't know—emptied them and then—"

"Jake, stop," he said, and something in his voice didn't body well. "Tell me: exactly how many bags were *left?*"

"Oh, um," I stammered, "I think, I guess, um, seven?"

You don't need a lie detector to see through that one.

"Jacob! Your mother *thought* you weren't telling the truth! How many meals have you skipped?" he demanded ... and I couldn't think fast enough to get out of it.

"Three, Dad. It's been three days," I said.

"And before that?" he asked. Parents. How *do* they guess these things?

"Three days before that." I could tell the speech was coming. There was a note of disappointment in his voice when he continued.

"Son, you *know* better than this! You have to take responsibility for your health—you aren't a little kid anymore," he said.

"Right. Sorry. I'm sorry, Dad." I felt guilty and defeated—and I was absolutely terrified he'd ask *why*. But he didn't. He sighed over the line instead.

"Well, that's that."

"But Dad! Someone's taken my food!" I reminded him.

"No one stole your food, son."

"But—" I started, but he interrupted me with the weirdest question:

"Jake, how are you sleeping?" It was so out-of-the-blue that it took the wind out of my sails.

"Uh, I don't know. I had a few restless nights, but what does that have to do with anything?" I could hear him switching the phone to his shoulder, and then behind him the screen door closing. When he spoke up again, he'd dropped his voice a bit.

"Do you remember when you were little and we used to find you all over the house sleepwalking?"

"Yeah, but how does that—"

"Do you know *why* you used to sleepwalk, Jake? Because you were hungry."

Now, maybe it was the lack of food, and maybe it was panic, but I was not seeing the connection.

"I'm not seeing the connection," I admitted.

"Think. You sleepwalk to look for food. You knew the bag was under your bed, and your subconscious mind led you right to it."

"Wait just a minute. You're trying to tell me that I got up last night and drank all three bags while I was *asleep*??"

"Three!" My dad exclaimed, and I realized I'd just given myself away. "You were going to try and make it another week on three bags? After you told me seven?"

"Oh. Um. Well—"

"You had better not tell your mother about this."

"Yes, sir," I said—as if I ever had any intention of doing *that*.

"Here's what we'll do, son," he said, even more quietly. It was clear to me by this time that he was avoiding my mother. He is, after all, a man of vision. "It's Wednesday night. I can't leave until Saturday, but you've consumed three bags in twenty-four hours, so you should be fine."

"Serious? I mean, Dad, I don't *feel* fine!" It was true. My stomach was rumbling and bucking and making a nuisance of itself. But my father just sighed.

"Jake, where else would the blood go?"

It was a good question. But it also gave me a sudden chilling vision of *Dracula*'s Van Helsing, who says the same thing a lot. He was right, though. There was just no other likely explanation. Apparently, he sensed my resignation, because he assumed a slightly more cheerful tone after that. It isn't like my dad to discipline over the phone. That's what long car rides home are for.

"Now, I will arrive early Sunday morning with a new supply. But listen to me, Jake: if this is an emergency, or becomes one, I can take off tomorrow and be there by sunset."

I hesitated. Part of me wanted to see him tomorrow, but I couldn't really say it was an emergency. His theory was pretty sound—it made perfect sense, in fact—and besides, I thought I might get less of an earful if he had three days to cool off.

"No, that's fine. It's not an emergency," I said. My dad ended the conversation reassuringly, but I hung up the phone feeling depressed and sick to my stomach. Still, I told myself, *it's only three days.*

It couldn't kill me.

Chapter 8

It was a terrible evening. For one thing, I knew I was going to catch it from Dad—for another, I'd have to leave early, just when things were starting to get interesting with Zsòfia. The only thing worse than thinking about Leonard squirreling into my territory was the awful pain in my stomach. And it didn't feel like an over-full tank, either. It felt like running on empty.

"Jake, dear? Your father just rang—" my aunt's voice drifted up the stairs. "He says you want to go home early?"

I was lying on the bed with a pillow over my face, and for a minute, I thought about suffocating myself.

"Ah, yeah. I mean—no. I don't *want* to, but I'm kind of feeling gross."

She hovered at my bedroom door like a big, purple butterfly.

"Gross?"

"Sick, Aunt Syl."

There. I said it. And at last, my aunt's life had purpose and meaning. For the next ten minutes she fluttered and fussed about my "nervous stomach," and by the time she left I was stuck with a heating pad, a hot-water bottle and more of that crap tea—in a thermos, by the bed.

"And I put a whole new roll of toilet paper in the bath, just in case!" Syl smiled and patted my head. I was ready to die. I wish my dad would have made something else up about my eating disorders. The bathroom joke was wearing a bit thin.

"Thanks," I muttered, mostly because that was the only way to get her out of my room. And then, I lay there and stared at the ceiling fan. It was seven in the evening, so I wasn't sleepy ... but even if I was, there was no chance of dozing off. My abdomen was doing a jig of some sort, cramping and burning. I actually cradled a pillow under it all night, and—I'm ashamed to admit—I actually *did* use the stupid heating pad. The worst of it finally quit after two in the morning, and I finally fell asleep.... But, after what felt like only ten minutes, I was shaken awake again by Aunt Syl.

"Jacob!" She sounded kind of panicked, and for a minute I thought the house was on fire or something.

"Wha—What? What is it?" I mumbled. I had turned around funny in the night and was lying parallel to the twin mattress, so my head and one arm were hanging off the side. When I got myself upright, I blinked in the absolutely blinding daylight and tried to process what was going on.

My aunt was in a half-crouch, her eyes wider (if possible) than I'd ever seen them. They were positively *lid-less*.

"Oh, Jacob! Oh *dear!*" She pressed her hands in a distraught sort of way, and I started worrying the cats had been murdered.

"Good grief, what's going on?" I asked, "Did someone die?"

"Die! Die!" she squeaked. "You're ill! We should call your father right now!"

"Um, hold up there a minute." I knew it was a bad idea to tell her I wasn't feeling well. I sat up and put on my very best thank-you-I'm-fine expression and tried again. "I'm not ill—are you? Shouldn't you be teaching right now?"

"Oh, Jacob," she said. The look of alarm wasn't going away, it was just softening into something a lot like pity. "It's five o'clock in the *afternoon!*"

This, you can imagine, caught me a bit off guard. I actually jumped off the mattress and stared around the room for a minute in dizzying disorientation.

"That can't be right! Wait—I was supposed to see Zsòfia this afternoon!" I actually picked up my alarm and shook it, thinking that would help or something.

"I know," my aunt said, "she called me and said you didn't come down. I thought you might have gone out!"

"She was *here?* Oh, man!" I smacked myself on the forehead and sat back down on the bed. Was there no end to my embarrassing moments? What was wrong with my body, anyhow?

My aunt, apparently mistaking this as "a turn for the worse" started examining my face like it was a slow-reacting chemical compound. She was doing that psychoanalytic thing, I'm sure of it.

"Syl—really, stop that. I'm fine. See, I was sick as a dog last night, so I slept really terrible. I had to catch up, that's all."

"Dear boy," she said, and that was the last coherent thing I understood because she'd just started speaking Professoreeze. Something about "adamant" and "pedantic" and "obfuscating" with some "enervated" and "ailing" thrown in. Suffice it to say the translation was something like: *you worried your aunt, you heedless, twitter-headed darling, you.* I had to spend so much time reassuring her of my health that I hardly had the energy to do what the occasion called for ... mainly, getting worked up and worried about *myself.*

In all my life (which, granted, hasn't been very long) I've never slept away an entire day like that. Sure, I'm nocturnal, but I'm not lazy ... and fifteen hours is a LONG TIME to be dead to the world. My aunt finally left, satisfied with the promise that I would come sit with her at dinner and demonstrate my wellness, so I took a shower. A really long shower. During which I tried to get my brain around some things, like the fact that it was Thursday night.

I *did* sit with my aunt. She stared at me a lot and I smiled a lot. It was sort of painful, but at least my stomach wasn't cramping. I even drank some of her tea.

"I can't believe I missed Zsòfia. She must think I'm an idiot," I muttered. I don't normally confide in Syl, but I was hoping she'd say more about her conversation with Zsòfia in the afternoon.

"There, now! Don't worry your head over it! Zsòfia is a *most* understanding young woman. I reminded her that you young boys can be very forgetful; and of course, she knows you have a *condition.*"

This was not reassuring.

"You—you told her I forgot?"

"I thought you must have, of course! Whoever would think you'd slept the day away!" she tittered. And this was true, actually. Who would think that?

"Oh great, that means she thinks I just blew her off!" I rubbed my face with my hands. "Can't you call and tell her I didn't do it on purpose?"

"That's very thoughtful, Jacob, dear. Here you are—" she handed me her cell phone and went back to the crossword.

"Um?" I stared at the phone.

"Didn't you want to touch base with her?"

I blinked. After all, that was practically a loaded question. Instead of answering I hunted the contacts list for her name. Ten minutes later, I was on the porch, waiting for Zsòfia to pick up. It was, I think, the longest twenty seconds of my life.

"'Allo?"

She had answered. Now what?

"I'msorryImissedyouIdidn'thearyouIthought—"

"Jacob? Is that you?"

Just answer the question, stupid, I thought.

"Uh, yes? I mean, yes, it is," I cleared my throat and tried again. "I'm so sorry—I didn't forget you were coming, honest! I just overslept. A lot. Well, sort of fourteen hours over, anyway...." And at this point my brain, which had just encouraged me to talk, was now begging me to shut up.

"I am very pleased that you did not forget," she said. "It was sweet for you to call me."

I wasn't sure how close sweet was to sexy. I hoped it was on the spectrum somewhere.

"Will you come tomorrow?"

"Yes, I am behind on my work."

"Oh. Right—well. I'll see you then?" I asked, hoping for maybe a smidge more than work chat. But I didn't get anything but a polite goodbye. Still, she was glad I called. She was coming the next day. This was good. The next important move was to make sure I actually woke up on time. I decided to tuck in early (and I was surprisingly tired anyhow), so I gave Syl her phone and got ready for bed.

I plodded upstairs and kicked my shoes off. I half thought of calling Henry, but headed into the bathroom instead to brush my teeth. At first, I was too busy moping about all the extra toilet paper to look in the mirror—but when I did, I was in for a shock.

Yes, I could still see myself (it was Henry's first question when I later told him about it). But I'm not sure I wanted to. It was no wonder Syl had freaked out about my health: I looked *awful*. I'm a blond from a family of blonds, but living in Virginia and being an avid swimmer/surfer makes me far from pale. I usually look tan and healthy and glowing and all that, but the face in the mirror was pale and drawn. Since the stomach pains had gone away, I assumed I was doing better, but I began having some serious doubts right about then. I poked at my face, the dark circles, the hollow expression, and rubbed my skin with my palms.... Nothing brought the blood to the surface, though. I couldn't even manage a red mark from pinching myself.

"Weird," I thought, but it was about to get a lot weirder. When I opened my mouth to brush my teeth, I was greeted with another surprise: those were not my teeth.

Well, they *were*. But only just. I mean, everyone has pointy canines—hold over from cavemen or whatever. But mine looked a lot more caveman than usual. *That's just not possible*, I assured myself. *Nope. They are not longer or sharper. It's the light.* That worked pretty well, so I tried self-delusion for the other symptoms, chalking them up to illness, nerves, and half the health problems I only pretend to have. All the same, I wasn't able to escape a nagging suspicion: for not *really* being a vampire, I was looking pretty undead, indeed. I climbed into bed with that unfriendly thought, and—despite my fourteen-hour respite the day before—fell asleep immediately.

There's no good way to keep track of dreams; you swear you've dreamt an hour and you've only been asleep for fifteen minutes, or you think you've had a quick little dream and suddenly it's morning. I don't really get the timetable, but the next thing I knew I was wide awake in the dark.

If I had been disoriented from waking at five in the afternoon, it was nothing compared to *this* piece of weirdness—first, I was not lying in bed. Second, I wasn't even in my room. In fact, for a panicky moment, I thought I wasn't even in the right house! Imagine how you would feel, standing barefoot in your shorts in someone else's living room. I stood that way for a few minutes, listening to my heart beating way out of rhythm and staring all around in the dark. Trust me, when you are disoriented, even night vision isn't much help and it took like ten minutes before my eyes rested on a familiar shape—a large stone basin my aunt bought from an art festival. I was in the TV room at the end of the first floor hallway. I let out a long breath I hadn't realized I'd been holding and rubbed my face with both hands. I couldn't believe it; there I was, standing stock still behind a micro-suede sofa in the middle of the night. A day earlier and I would have sworn I'd long outgrown sleepwalking.

Hunger walk, I thought. Dad was right. The clock on the mantle said 2 am, but to be honest, I wasn't the least bit tired. Not anymore (not after all that sleep). Besides, there I was in front of a television and all.... I hopped over the edge of the sofa and settled onto the cushions, but unfortunately, Byron was tucked into one of them and I flopped him onto the floor.

"Sorry, cat," I said, and then I reached out to stroke his back, but the strangest thing happened. He *hissed* at me. And I don't mean your average I'm-irritated-that-you-sat-on-me hiss, but a full-on, teeth-bared, claws-raised growl. He leapt onto the coffee table in front of me, spitting and slicing and looking for all the world like a recoiled, spring-loaded scratch factory. You might wonder what *my* next move was, and if you guessed "backwards over the sofa and up the stairs," you'd be right. Why? I was petrified. No, not of the cat—what's a few scratches to a fast healer? I was shocked by Byron's reaction to me, but I was way more freaked out by my reaction to Byron. You see, in that split second that exists before reason catches up with response, my first impulse was *to bite him*.

Chapter 9

I HAD NEVER REACTED THAT WAY TO ANYTHING, EVER. I'd been mad before, sure, and I'd been hungry before, too—but never did that lead to *such* a powerful feeling. I shut myself in the bedroom and locked the door, but the feeling was still there—a terrible, throbbing desire to eat *something* had become a desire to eat *anything*. I'm still a little shaken, looking back; I'm a cat lover, after all, and yet I could hear Byron's heartbeat. I think I could even *smell* him. And I couldn't shake the feeling that Byron knew it, that he sensed all was not right in my world, that I was changing somehow and becoming a little dangerous. I crawled back into bed without working it all out, and didn't sleep much after that. My pop is a smart guy. And persuasive, too. But I was having trouble buying his night-eating theory. Unfortunately, without a better explanation, the questions just went on revolving around my brain until daybreak.

In a way, it was probably good I didn't go back to sleep, because I wouldn't have woken up in time to see

Zsòfia. All the same, I felt so weak and looked so terrible that I didn't dare go down until after my aunt had left for work. My haggard appearance would have sent her into conniptions, and it wasn't making me very happy either. My eyes had dark shadows under them, my cheeks looked hollow and pinched, and my skin was a really awful color—it had gone kind of grayish under my tan. My only consolation was that, if I looked that bad on Friday, I was bound to look too terrible to yell at by the time my dad arrived on Sunday.

I dragged my sad self to the library sofa and flopped onto it with a magazine. I was too tired to read, but I thought the pictures might help me stay awake until our appointed rendezvous. I was wrong, of course. I had been asleep twenty minutes when I heard the door opening. I know I should have gotten up or something, but the effort seemed too gargantuan.

" 'Allo, Jacob," Zsòfia said. She had her arms full of books and a sack of some kind. She was so busy with these that she didn't look at me right off, but when she did, she parted her lips in surprise.

"Oh—but you are very ill!" she said. It was so NOT the way my aunt said it ... so wonderfully wonderful and feminine that I kind of melted into the couch and embraced my condition.

"I *so* am," I said. It wasn't that I was playing it up, after all. I just wasn't playing it off.

"Oh, dear!" she put down her things and pulled a stool over to the couch. Then she petted and made over me like I was a two year old, which is counterproductive if the image you are trying to put forth is athletic-desirable-available-male. But I just couldn't help it! I was feeling terrible and exhausted, and I wanted nothing more than to lie in a sunny spot and have her speak Hungarian. I have no idea what she was calling me, in retrospect, but she stroked my hair and said all sorts of nice sounding words. If I'd had the anatomy for it, I'd have purred.

"What could make you feel better, Jacob?" she asked finally.

"Oh, well, my parents are coming this Sunday with special stuff," I said softly. "Then I'll be okay."

To be honest, I was starting to lose my fight with sleep again, and I was trying not to say anything incriminating.

"Sunday! You are leaving on Sunday?"

"Mm-hmm. Ran out of food." Which was exactly what I was trying to not say. I snapped my eyes back open, but it was too late to recall it.

"Food? Ah! I shall make you well, then." Zsòfia had been clutching the strap of a small canvas bag, and she drew it nearer. "See? I have brought you food!"

"Oh—er, no. See, I can only eat special food," I said.

"I have special food," she said, and for a minute, I started to wonder exactly what was *in* there. Out came a Tupperware bowl, full of little biscuits.

"Yes, your aunt, she tells me about this," she said, and then, to my dismay, she listed all the odd (and complicated) ingredients my father made up so that my aunt wouldn't bother cooking for me. I admit, I was shocked to discover that stuff like this actually existed, but apparently they can be had at health food stores, because Zsòfia—who was obviously more adventurous in the kitchen than Aunt Syl—had *made* something with them.

"Wow," is what I said. *This is SO not good*, is what I thought. Zsòfia held it before me. As if I weren't already nauseous enough.

"Aren't you hungry?" she asked. She was sort of leaning forward, and her big, dark eyes were looking right into mine.

I didn't answer. The problem was that I *was* hungry—terribly, horribly, desperately hungry. But to say yes would be to invite the cake-like stuff, which would probably go a good ways towards killing me at that point (not sure how much of my innards still functioned on solids).

"No, no," I managed finally. She leaned a little closer. Nearly touching me.

I was tired and all, but I wasn't *that* tired.

"Surely you are hungry?" she asked. "Did you not say that you have run out of food?" She started petting my hair again, and the sensation made me feel tingly.

"Oh yeah—I mean, *no!*" I said in confusion. "I, uh, only meant that I would run out *soon*. It's upstairs."

"With the blood?" she asked. And yes, under normal circumstances I should have registered this with shock. But, it was also at this point that she started tracing her fingers over my face. I was already tired, but this made my eyes turn suddenly heavy and it was only with heroic effort I kept them open at all.

"With the blood," I said. I was starting to feel a little foggy in the head.

"Well, you rest then, Jacob dear," she whispered. It might as well have been a command—my lack of sleep, my empty stomach, and the slow, quiet tracing of her fingers over my face put me out like a light.

I awoke hours later to the strange sensation of someone standing over me. I snapped my eyes open—but there was no one there. The room was darkened, lit only by a standing lamp in the corner. Which meant, of course, that it was night. I started up into a sitting position and blinked at the wall clock. It was almost eight in the evening.

"Oh, good *Lord*," I groaned, putting my face in my hands. I'd fallen asleep on Zsòfia. "You are awake?"

I lifted my head in shock to see Zsòfia in the doorway.

"You're still here?" I asked. There's charm for you. She shrugged lightly and walked into the room.

"I have been studying," she said. This was mixed relief.

"Where is Aunt Syl?"

"Your aunt, she went to get your sister from camp for the weekend—yes? You knew that?" she asked. I half nodded. I couldn't remember if I knew that or not.

"Oh—right. Did she come home first?" That was a stupid question, since she must have. I was about to try and correct my clumsy speech, but my eyes had just fallen upon the blue cooler. My blue cooler. It was on the floor at Zsòfia's feet.

"Ah," she said, following my gaze. "Your aunt said you had lost it, but she found it in your room. I was to tell you when you woke."

The panic must have been visible on my face—if my aunt knew it was all gone she would think I'd have had numerous transfusions at her house. Zsòfia leaned down and touched my arm softly.

"It is all right," she whispered, almost in my ear. "She did not look. *She does not know.*"

She does not know what? I thought, staring. I'd been awake for all of two minutes and I'd just had heart-attack news, because a comment like that could only mean that Zsòfia *had* looked.... And why would she? I swallowed hard and tried evasion.

"Yeah, uh, its better she doesn't know. About my transfusions, I mean. She worries, you know?" I've heard Lizzy say things like this a hundred times, but from me it sounded utterly unconvincing.

"Yes, *I* understand," Zsòfia said. There is a quality in the way some people talk that expresses way more than the words they use—I don't know how it works, but right then I felt like Zsòfia was broadcasting something. It made my skin feel hot and cold at the same time.

"You—do? And my aunt ...?" was all I managed to say. She was leaning over me again—I mean *way* over me, so that her right hand rested on the cushion above my head and her hair pooled in marvelous waves on my chest and neck. I will spare you my exact thoughts. Something about the cooler, and my condition, mixed up with the fact that I hadn't kissed a girl since eighth grade—but Zsòfia wasn't aiming for my lips. She leaned forward and kissed my forehead. I was momentarily saved from embarrassment, but the sensation that replaced it was much worse. If you haven't done it in a while, allow me to remind you that kissing someone's forehead generally puts your neck directly in front of their mouth. Let me also remind you that it was now dark in the room, and that the impulse from the night before was returning with a vengeance. Zsòfia's throat actually brushed my lips, and I heard it—her heartbeat.

Let it never be said that I have no will power. Let it never be said that I'm not a praying man. I scarcely dared to breathe until she was safely seated on the footstool again.

"You seem nervous," she said.

Duh. But I had clamped my mouth shut and so couldn't talk very well.

"I wonder why you are nervous…. Are you nervous because you like me? Or …" she trailed off, but before I had the chance to answer she took me by the chin and turned my face toward hers. "Or is it because you have something to tell me?"

This situation was becoming very strange. Kind of sexy, but strange all the same. She kept staring at me with those deep eyes, and I tried to do some quick sums—the cooler, the fact it was empty, the food she made, the kiss, the question.

What was going on here?

"Jacob," she said at last. "Do you keep secrets?"

"Secrets?" This is my favorite tactic—useful for answering angry parents, siblings, and teachers. When in doubt, just repeat the last word the other person says.

"Yes. Everyone has a secret, I think. Everyone has something that no one knows about them," she paused and leaned away again, casting her eyes downward. "There is much you do not know about me. There is much I do not know about you."

"About you?" I asked, sticking to the only safe ground I could find.

"Yes!" she said this with more energy than I expected, "Yes. And yet we make a guess, don't we? But we never know until we are told."

She leaned on her knee and looked at me sideways—a schoolgirl kind of look. I was having trouble keeping up with the sheer variety of ways she could be totally hot.

"Jacob, do you have something to tell me?" she asked again.

"Me?" This was not one of my best moments. I was going to have to venture beyond parroting in a minute or risk something worse. "I don't know—I'm not sure what you mean."

"I see," she said. And suddenly, her manner completely changed. The dewy warmth had gone and something different—not colder, but farther away—replaced it. It was the reverse of what happened during my "going away" dinner, only now I was getting shut out instead of let in, and I didn't like it at all. When she spoke again, she sounded hurt and disappointed.

"You know, I had something I wished to tell you. But perhaps I am wrong," she said.

"Whoa—wait! You—you have something to tell *me*?" I asked. She was a gothic historian. She was a vampire scholar. She was digging me. What *else* was there?

"Please, wait!" I begged.

She shook her head.

"We cannot share secrets if only one person tells their secrets."

"But I want to share! I'm good at sharing!" I insisted. This, I know, was bad. Bad as in going against everything I'd been taught to NOT say about my "condition." But Zsòfia turned and looked at me over her shoulder. There was a glistening in her eyes.

"I will share things with you if you will also share," she said.

"Share? *Things?*" I swallowed with some difficulty.

"It will be a sign of trust between us. Our secret."

My brain was doing woozy somersaults. Secret. Share. Things.

"Zsòfia—" I started, but I didn't say anything else. I didn't have time to. She had just descended upon me and kissed me.

For real.

I think I died. Because when I heard her voice again, it was coming from far away through a weird, dreamy haze.

"Tomorrow you will meet me," she said. "At midnight. In the Cemetery Chapel."

"Absolutely," I said.

And then, she left. I didn't see her to the door. I didn't even get up. I just sat there on the couch and starred at where she'd been standing. Somewhere in my brain, a faint voice was trying to tell me this was not a smart move. But pretty much the rest of me was feeling painfully excited. For once in his life, Henry was totally spot-on. She wanted a vampire? She got one. Zsòfia had all this knowledge, and now she wanted to have *me*.

And let's face it, I was only too happy to oblige.

Chapter 10

I REMAINED MOSTLY IMMOBILE ON THE LIBRARY SOFA UNTIL I heard the crunch of tires on gravel. My aunt was home, bringing Lizzy for her weekend respite from acting camp. I sighed and got prepared for the onslaught—which was good, because Lizzy started talking even before she got through the door.

"Aunt Syl says you've been making up to that grad student the whole time! I can't believe you're that stupid, I mean—JAKE!" Lizzy had just come around the corner with her gear—which she dropped on the floor at the sight of me. "You look *terrible!*"

"It's nice to see you, too," I said. Her week among theater people clearly made her more dramatic than ever.

"I'm serious!" Lizzy looked over her shoulder to see if our aunt had followed her into the study. "Really, Jake—this is the worst I've ever seen you!"

"Look, Liz—"

"Is that your cooler? What the heck is it doing down here? Syl's just checking the mail—she'll be here any minute!"

"It's fine," I muttered, trying to smack her hands away.

"Let me see in there—I *know* you've been skipping meals. You're absolutely gross looking, and I'm calling Dad *right now*!"

"Well, you're a little late," I said wearily. I was not in the mood for a harangue. "I've already called and fessed up. They'll be here Sunday."

"Sunday! Jake, I don't think you can wait until then!"

"All right, drama queen. It's not like I'm dying," I said. Lizzy crossed her arms and looked at me through her just-like-my-mother eyebrows.

"Are you sure?" She asked. I'll admit, that's not a question a person likes to hear.

"Geez, do I really look that bad?" I asked.

"When's the last time you looked in a mirror? Aunt Syl will have a coronary."

"Relax, Sunday's only a day away," I said, and for some reason, that brought Lizzy back around to her first question.

"And are we planning to dally with Helga all Saturday, then?" she asked.

"Zsòfia. And none of your business."

"So you *are* going to see her! What is it, lunch in the park?"

"Hardly," I grumped, feeling that our rendezvous was nothing to make light of.

"Oh, come off it. What could she possibly see in you?"

"You know, you are really a confidence booster," I said, mostly to avoid telling her what I actually thought she saw in me. I really just wanted to be left alone so I could think about what was going to happen the next day. My aunt had come in at last, but through the back door closer to the car park. I called down the hall to the kitchen and said goodnight. Lizzy intervened to keep her from coming to say the same in person, and I went up to my room.

But Lizzy was right. I looked worse. My eyes, which are normally blue, seemed almost gray, and my white blond hair actually looked darker than my face. I was still assessing the damage when Lizzy pushed the door open and tossed the empty cooler on the bed.

"If you knew you were going to stay longer, why didn't you ration?" she asked.

"Well," I sighed. "I tried. Had enough until Wednesday. Then I guess I drank it at night in my sleep."

"Somnambulism," Lizzy said.

"God bless you."

"Oh, you dork—it means sleepwalking."

"Then say sleepwalking. Have you been playing Scrabble with Aunt Syl again?"

Lizzy gave me a dirty look.

"Come on, do you really think you did all that in your sleep? I mean, maybe someone took the rest," she said.

"Who, the blood pirates? That's the dumbest thing I've ever heard," I snarked, which wasn't totally fair since that had been my first idea, too.

"Oh yeah? Did you count the empty containers?" she asked.

"What for?"

"Maybe your pal Helga took off with them, huh? She's Romanian, right? She's probably a vampire, too."

"Come off it, you ate dinner with her; she's not snacking on O positive. And, I might add, her name is *Zsòfia* and she is from *Hungary*."

"Well, whatever. Either way, *I* think she's probably a dangerous loony—she hangs out with you, after all—and I'm not letting you out of my sight until Dad gets here."

I sighed. She was going to make this all rather difficult.

"Shouldn't you be yakking about how great camp is or something?" I asked, sinking into the bed. She didn't answer. She was unzipping the cooler. I caught the strap and pulled it away.

"Hey! I just want to count!"

I stood up with an effort and took her by both hands.

"You are going bye-bye now. I'm tired and hungry and I need to sleep. Anyway, you're an amateur actor, not an amateur sleuth." I pushed her out the door. Well, honestly, I just gave her a half-hearted noodge and she left. Either way, I got some peace. I barely managed to undress, though, and slipped into bed still wearing my T-shirt. I didn't sleep walk that night, though. I slept like the dead.

When I woke up, it was utterly silent. It was a fuzzy, stifled kind of silence—and the light was fuzzy and stifled looking, too. I rolled over with effort to look out the window and saw something I typically don't: dawn. This was disconcerting, except that I was happy to be waking up at all. I actually felt like I'd been hit by a truck, and my whole body ached and complained as I made my way to the bathroom. I fumbled with the light and was greeted with the next terrible surprise of the morning. I looked like an under-exposed Polaroid. My eyes were washed out, my skin was papery white, even my fingernails looked white. When I went to brush my teeth, my gums were bluish rather than pinkish and seemed to have shrunk back over my teeth—which were definitely more pronounced. It was worse than looking ill; I looked positively frightening. There was *no way* my aunt could see me like this—in fact, I couldn't even let Lizzy see me like this. I decided that, if I were to meet Zsòfia at all—Zsòfia, who had something to share, who had secrets, and who dug me—then I'd have to leave before anyone else got up.

I wasn't sure where I would go. Aunt Syl had been pushing the museums on me since I got there, but I didn't have the energy for that. I actually thought about going straight to the cemetery chapel; if I was lucky, I could find a place inside to sleep. I picked up one of the brochures about the chapel's stained glass and checked the address. It wasn't that far away. I tossed it back on the bed and put on a ball cap, a shirt with a high collar and a pair of dark sunglasses. The result made me look less like an albino vampire and more like a—well, like a freak with a hat and dark glasses. I left a note on the counter, saying I was going to see the sights (which was true, kind of) and left.

The graveyard was easy to get to if you walked through the park. It should have been pleasant, but to be honest, I don't even remember if the sun was out. It was almost like I was seeing things in black and white—as if being washed out myself made everything else look that way. My focus was on walking; it's like I'd forgotten how to do involuntary stuff; I was practically coaching my muscles to do their normal gig: *leg up, leg down, heel, toe.* I must have looked like a goose-stepping moron. And yes, it has since occurred to me that I'm an idiot. Anyone in their right mind would have guessed something was *very* wrong, but I had my brain trained on one thing—and it's probably not what you think. Somewhere in the back of my muddled head an idea was starting to jiggle around. Zsòfia clearly wasn't epilemic—but she had a secret. She also had a book about vampires from Switzerland ... *and* she guessed what I was and thought it was groovy and sexy. Okay, it is what you think. But in addition to the fact that I was totally infatuated with her, I was also curious: what if, just maybe, she knew more about my condition than *I* did?

The "chapel" didn't actually turn out to be much of a chapel at all. The brochures made it look big and impressive, but it was really a smallish mausoleum kind of place, not big enough for real church services. No one was around, but the sign said it closed at 7 pm—closed and probably locked, too. It was dim inside, but the whole back wall was a giant stained glass window depicting Greek-looking people doing Greek-looking stuff. It was so huge that the figures were bigger than I was—they virtually loomed in the tiny little place. But I wasn't really there to critique the art; there were six pews, three on each side, covered in red cushions. Comfortable looking cushions. I almost cried. And then I found the furthest, dimmest corner, curled up and went to sleep.

When I woke, it was very dark, and I'd forgotten where I was. I'd also forgotten that I was scrunched on a pew, so in starting awake, I fell face-forward onto the floor.

"Crap," I muttered, and it echoed a little. The air had gotten chilly and the place seemed creepy and unfriendly in the dark. The chapel was only dimly lit by a security light near the door, and it gave an electric orange kind of glow. Not exactly inviting. On the other hand, it meant Zsòfia wouldn't see what a freak I'd become. I took a breath and sat on the nearest pew; it was about 10:05; I had two hours to kill and was beginning to get a serious case of nerves.

Apart from Henry, no one outside my family knew the whole weird truth of my "condition." Heck, even Aunt Syl didn't know. My dad had always more or less committed me to a half-truth, even with the hospital people (and that made him sort of unpopular at times). It wasn't lying exactly; it's just that there was still a lot about me that his theory didn't quite cover. Transfusions were one thing. Eating other people's plasma and platelets, well, that was another. And now, here I was, hanging out in a graveyard and preparing to tell the most beautiful woman on God's green earth that I was on a pretty literal liquid diet. How exactly was I going to *do* that?

Hi, I'm a vampire, sort of? Too stupid sounding.

So, I've got this blood disorder? Too lame.

I'm the real live Bela Lugosi? Right, like she'd never heard that before. She wanted to share secrets. She wanted to share sexy secrets—I was *sure* of it. And if she had something good, then I'd better take it up a notch.

Then again, what *did* she want to share? *The Vampire Bible* was a bit chilling and bizarre—but maybe there was more to it. Sexual politics, my foot. I'd spent most of my life not thinking too much about my kind of weird ... but maybe Zsòfia knew something? What? And—more importantly—what did she want from me? I grinned a little. She wanted me....

Unless? Unless maybe, just maybe, *she wanted to be a vampire herself* ...?

And with that unfriendly thought, I started to really freak out.

Chapter 11

I DIDN'T KNOW WHERE THAT AWFUL IDEA CAME FROM, BUT there it was. You see it in the movies, don't you? What if Zsòfia didn't *want* me, want me? What if she wanted to *be* me? What if she'd brought me out here to—? What if she really did take my rations, so I would be hungry enough to—? I couldn't quite bring myself to complete the thought, and the next moment a rapping on the door made me jump out of my skin.

"Jacob?" Zsòfia's muffled voice came from outside. "Are you here?"

I swallowed. Did I let her in?

Yup.

"Hang on," I said. Someone had, in fact, bolted the door ... probably never noticed me passed out in there. I slid the catch aside and the electric orange light fell on Zsòfia ... who had come prepared. There was a set of criminal-looking tools in her hand.

"Ah, good. I do not have to break the lock," she said, putting them away. And yeah, that gave me the teeniest start.

"You—really? You would have broken in?"

"It is so very important," she said, smiling warmly, "that we have privacy."

My head went in six different directions thinking of all the things you need privacy for … ending with a quick prayer that vamping wasn't the one she meant.

"Well, ah, come in," I said. Awkwardly. I mean, it wasn't like I lived in the graveyard. She slid past with a rather ungainly looking knapsack and looked around. Then she started lighting candles, and I started saying dumb things.

"Romantic dinner for two?" I said, which was stupid.

"I mean for one," I corrected, which (given my last thought) was stupid *and* suspicious.

"I mean, not for me. I'm not eating. Anything. At all." Which was stupid and pointless. I opted to stop talking.

"It is to set the mood," Zsòfia said. "Now Jacob, we are going to share a secret."

"Right," I said, cautiously.

"And you will tell me …?" she asked expectantly.

"Right," I said again, but how could I say that? It was so *wrong*!

Zsòfia tilted her head.

"You are nervous again."

"Ah, no, I'm not," I lied.

"Yes, you are tense—let me see," she walked around behind me and began to massage my shoulders. Which was kind of unfair. I felt my eyelids getting heavy under the pressure of her fingertips.

"It is a matter of trust between us," she whispered in my ear. "We must have perfect trust."

"Trust," I repeated. "You, um, you trust me, too, right?"

"It depends," she said, and her fingers pinched for a minute. "You see, you must prove yourself. You do want to prove yourself, don't you?"

To be honest, I did. I'd skipped out on my aunt and Lizzy, who were probably freaking out and alerting the neighborhood watch. I'd skipped meals, and then I'd dragged my sorry self across town to hide in a graveyard. I was behaving like a B-movie character, and I'm not even a Goth. So yes, I wanted to prove myself to her more than anything I could think of at that moment ... which, with her fingers working up my neck, wasn't much.

"Yeah—yeah I do. But, well, I'm not sure how," I said. She stopped and leaned close to my ear.

"Tell me. Tell me a secret."

A silent pause. My heart was beating double, and I could feel her breath on my neck. I decided to take the plunge.

"All right. Zsòfia, I'm—well, I'm a vampire."

And frankly, it sounded just as dumb out loud as it did in my head. Why can't I think of more poignant ways of saying these things—you know, something deep and romantic and poetic or *something*.

Zsòfia didn't say anything for a long time. She was still standing behind me, but I was afraid to look up. Finally, she made a noise that sounded like a cross between a sigh and a bark, like suppressed excitement.

"I am so glad, Jacob. Stay right here, and don't look. I have something to share with you," Her voice was almost breathless. And I was pretty breathless, too.

"You have something to share?" I asked, half-turning, but she snapped her fingers loudly.

"Don't look! I will give you something when I am ready."

Now my heart was up in my eyeballs somewhere. Give me something? What something? I heard her rummaging in the bag. When she returned, I tried to face her but she steadied my head with her hand.

"Not yet, not yet, Jacob," she said. "I would like you to guess what secret I want to share with you."

Great. She was going to make *me* say it.

"I think—I think you stole the blood bags from my cooler," I said, talking faster than I meant to. I could feel her warm fingers caressing the nape of my neck.

"And why would I do this?" she asked—cooed, more like. I bit my lip; I didn't want to make it sound too over-dramatic. (I get enough of that crap from Lizzy.)

"Because ... you wanted to know for sure." A gentle squeeze on my shoulder.

"Go on," she said. Her voice sounded strangely tight.

"Um, because you wanted the things you study to be real. And—" No. I wasn't going to make that suggestion.

"What else, Jacob?" The fingers at my neck held a little firmer. "Why did I bring you here?"

Her voice was tense and high-pitched now, and I was beginning to get panicky again.

"You—Zsòfia, do you want to *be* a vampire??" I asked, gulping. *Please say no, please say no.*... After all,

I didn't even know if epilemia was catching. And who would want a life as complicated as mine anyhow?

Zsòfia's fingers stopped moving and there was a long, silent pause. But when she finally spoke, all the humor and warmth had completely gone from her voice.

"I am no vampire lover," she snapped. "I am a vampire *hunter*!"

And this, you might know, was followed by the very loud crack of a very heavy object connecting with my very muddled head.

Earlier that day, I felt like I'd been hit by a truck. When I woke up this time, I felt like one had run over my face. A roaring pain was running relays between my ears and coming to consciousness was no picnic. When I finally opened my eyes, I found that I could not move. At first I thought I'd been paralyzed. But no. I had been tied up. To the altar.

"Um—Zsòfia?" I asked. *Vampire hunter.* Funny, I hadn't thought of that. I didn't hear anything, so I tried to free myself. But I was weak—weaker than I've ever been in my life—and I couldn't budge.

"Awake?" Zsòfia's voice floated from overhead. I didn't like this voice—I mean, it was the same voice in a way, but it was not seductive or sweet or fascinating. It was downright scary.

"What *are* you doing?" I asked. "You hit me over the head—why, *why* am I tied to this thing?"

"You are a vampire," she said.

"Ah, no, I'm not."

"You are. I know it—I thought so when I saw the blood. I stole the rest to see what would happen to you, and then I knew. But," she walked away again, "I had to make sure."

"You haven't made sure of anything! You just, just," I shut up and struggled against the rope a bit more. The trouble was that I had just given my word, and that's pretty good evidence. Still, I could have been lying to impress her. If she was so smart, why didn't she think of that?

"Come on—this isn't funny. I'm your professor's nephew for crying out loud! How could I be a vampire?" This received no response. She was digging in the bag again. I noticed that there were candles all around the altar now and little vials of holy water and who knows what else. I couldn't see what she was doing, so I craned my neck to one side.

"Zsòfia, listen, you really need to untie me *right now*. That blood was for transfusions—you saw my kit and the needle, right? I don't *drink* it—"

"You don't need transfusions. You do drink it. You feed on the blood of the innocent," she said. And this was beginning to feel like a bad movie.

"What? I do *not* feed on the blood of innocents!" I shouted, which was true. I feed on the blood of blood donors—innocent and guilty don't enter into it.

"You stalk the living to feed the dead. You are a menace and a threat to mankind," she continued.

"I do *not* stalk! And I am *not* dead!" I yelled, "I have a pulse! I grew two inches last year! I'm turning seventeen—I'm *alive*!" Granted, I was looking pretty bad at that moment, but still. "Come on, let me up, and I'll prove it!!"

"You will never get up again. You will not be permitted to hunt and slay for your food." I thought that was way over the top—*everybody* hunts and slays for their food. Some just do the hunting at grocery stores and leave the slaying to the slaughterhouse.

"All right, I've had enough!" I shouted, trying not to sound like I was three degrees from panic meltdown. "You steal my stuff, you lure me out here, you hit me on the head, and now you are accusing me of all sorts of weird stuff. Let me up right now!"

I had begun to understand that for whatever vampire-killer book she was using, she had to set up a kind of ritual. With each successive trip to the knapsack, she brought back something else—crosses, books, candles, vials, etc. But the last things she took out made my heart skip a beat. On the pew just across from me was a grisly collection: a sharpened stake, a large mallet, and a butcher knife.

"Oh my God!" I chirped. Panic meltdown complete. "What are *those*?"

Zsòfia didn't answer, but she came back and split my shirt with a pen knife to expose my chest. I think I actually stopped breathing altogether right about then. Then she picked up her Bible and started reading parts in Hungarian while sprinkling my chest with the holy water. I thought she would be moved by the fact that it didn't start sizzling or anything, but not so. I listened to her mumbling and decided I'd better do some praying of my own—I don't recall the exact wording but it went something like this: *Hi, God, it's Jake. Please send the cavalry. If you don't, I hope you're happy to see me. Amen.* I had just finished a few renditions of this when she returned with the stake. And—oddly enough—a permanent marker.

"Hold still," she commanded. Then, she placed the point over where my heart *should* be, and would have been if it wasn't in my throat, and marked the place with a red X. Any fortitude I had left deserted me, and I started screaming like a little girl.

"Help! Help—Anybody!! Help!" I shrieked. You'd think that would have roused some pity or anger or *something*, but she was performing her solemn duty and would not be moved. I kept it up until she got the mallet, and then I was too busy hyperventilating to do much else. She placed the stake firmly over my heart and raised the mallet, and to be honest, if you've never stared at death like that you wouldn't get it even if I explained it to you. It's nerve shattering, it's absolutely terrifying. It's never-going-to-go-to-prom-to-college-tomorrow-today-you-die. There it is: the end of your life on this planet poised over your beating heart.

But, as you've probably guessed since I'm writing this, the mallet never actually fell. I closed my eyes waiting for it, but instead of the terrible sound I *thought* I was going to hear, I heard a voice shouting.

"Drop it, sister, or I'll put this needle right through your rib cage!"

I snapped my eyes open. Zsòfia was standing stock still and staring at the door. I could just barely see, but it was Lizzy—Lizzy and a very strange-looking weapon.

Chapter 12

"Don't make another move," Lizzy said. As she got closer, I could see that she held, of all things, the needle from the transfusion kit loaded onto what looked like a crossbow.

"What are you doing here?" Zsòfia demanded. "I am stopping the vampire—go away!"

"Vampire? Ha! *You're* the vampire!" Lizzy said, and I admit, I was a little fuddled. I mean, Zsòfia had the stake and I was the ghastly one on the altar. She didn't look like the vampire in this scenario at all.

"I'm no vampire, you silly girl! I am a vampire hunter. I am killing the vampire!"

"No," Lizzy said, coming still closer and pointing the needle at Zsòfia's chest. "*I'm* the vampire hunter. This needle is filled with holy water and I'm about to put it through you!"

"Put it through *him*, then, if you hunt the vampire!" Zsòfia cried, but she seemed a little shaken.

"Him? You cannot possibly think *that* is a vampire? He's my apprentice. He's *bait*."

"No—he exhibits all the signs!" Zsòfia said a little frantically.

"Because I told him to!" Lizzy shook her ponytail with dramatic flair. "We're *actors*. Don't you get it? We had to draw you out."

"Actors?"

"Of course. I knew *you* were a vampire as soon as I met you. Hungary's full of 'em." Lizzy said emphatically. With a twinge of irritation I noted that she was enjoying herself—my sister playing a dazzling part while I had a stake hovering over my chest.

"Look at his face! His skin! His teeth!" Zsòfia cried. I instinctively pursed my lips shut over the evidence.

"Clever makeup. Plastic and plaster—it's theater, after all. But you; you're the real deal. And I'm going to rid the world of your kind!" Lizzy poked the needle toward Zsòfia who was now sufficiently alarmed to drop the mallet and move away.

"Me! What signs do I have? I am not pale or sickly!" Zsòfia said emphatically, but the needle-gun was obviously making her nervous.

"Oh? You look pretty fair-skinned to me. And here you are, luring a young boy into a graveyard in the middle of the night! You have tied him up so you can sink your teeth into him!"

"What?" Zsòfia cried, but her mind seemed to be wrapping its way around the awkwardness of her situation.

"Give me one reason why I shouldn't plug you with holy water," Lizzy said, and I gotta admit, she looked kind of scary.

"Because," Zsòfia was looking really alarmed now. "Because why would I try to kill a vampire if I was a vampire?"

"Eliminate the competition," Lizzy said advancing. Zsòfia backed toward the exit.

"No, see, I have all the books and the holy water and everything!"

Lizzy hesitated a moment.

"Jake," she asked. "Did she tell you she was a vampire?"

"Um, no," I said.

"See—listen to the boy!" Zsòfia said.

"Sure, *now* you're on my side," I barked.

"You *really* aren't a vampire?" Lizzy asked. Zsòfia's eyes were still on the needle-gun.

"Really and truly. I am a hunter," she said.

Lizzy slowly lowered the needle.

"Is that a fact? Well, you really suck at it. You almost killed somebody."

The import of those words seemed to have a real effect—Zsòfia looked at me as if waking from a dream, but to be honest, I was much too angry to register what the look meant.

"Go on," my sister said, waving the needle again, "get out of here. Geez—you ought to be ashamed of yourself! You almost staked your advisor's nephew."

"You—you will not tell her?" Zsòfia asked. Lizzy turned on her and, quite frankly, she looked terrifying.

"You FREAK—get out of here before I decide to shoot you for stupidity!" It was pretty convincing, too, because Zsòfia made for the door without taking her stuff. Lizzy peeked out the casement and made sure she was gone before coming back to me.

"Jake—are you okay?"

"I'm tied to an altar! How could I possibly be okay?"

"Besides that? I mean, you're still all in one piece and all?"

"Yeah, I think," I said. Lizzy put her "weapon" down and started cutting through the ropes. I lay there, totally exhausted with the effort of being scared out of my wits, staring at the stake and mallet where they lay on the floor. Just a piece of wood and a hammer, but I don't think I'll ever get the image out of my head.

When Lizzy got me loose, we had another problem. I couldn't walk very well. It had been more than six full days since I'd had a meal. I was starving. To death. Lizzy propped me up and explained why she'd come.

"I counted the bags. Like I told *you* to do. Three were missing."

"Well—but how was I supposed to know?" I muttered, watching her pack up all the vampire hunter crap as evidence against Zsòfia.

"Because, dimwit, no grad student goddess would be into you. I mean, really."

I grimaced.

"Well—but how did you know where I went?"

"I didn't," She shoved the needle into the side pocket. "Aunt Syl and I hunted all the museums for you—we were still out well past eleven. But when I checked your cooler, I found the brochure. Figured I'd rig the needle on a theater prop just in case."

"In case she was a vampire?"

"Oh geez, Jake, there aren't any vampires—just stupid people. Well, and you, my dummy older brother. Now move, we gotta get out of here."

She's the smart one, Lizzy. Unfortunately, she's not the strong one, and my legs were like jelly. She half scooted, half dragged, half carried me home. Of course, in a college town on Saturday night, that doesn't really raise suspicion.... Besides, by the time we reached the house, we were both too exhausted to care what anyone thought. Lizzy even broke down and recruited my aunt to get me up the stairs. I don't know exactly how well that went, though, because I was getting pretty lightheaded. I do know that when they got me on the bed, my aunt went down to call my parent's cell phone ... and Lizzy, well, Lizzy tried to get me to bite her.

"Gross," I said. I had only one eye open, but I could see she was worried—maybe even scared. I must have looked just terrible.

"Jake, just some—just take some! They won't get here till tomorrow!" She was a little frantic, and it's always possible that she would have convinced me sooner or later, but I passed out right about then. The rest was narrated to me a few days later.

Apparently, I sort of slumped forward in a heap, and Lizzy had to wrestle me back onto the pillows. She picked up my wrist to place it at my side, and my skin was cold, so she checked my pulse. Now, Lizzy is usually the level-headed one, but since she couldn't *find* a pulse, she freaked out a little. Actually, the way I hear it from my aunt, she freaked out *a lot*. (She likes me, she really likes me.) My aunt was just hanging up the phone and Lizzy slammed into her, pulling and screaming and saying a lot of incoherent things about my being dead.

And, as it turns out, my aunt is rather better in a pinch than I would have given her credit for. I don't know if it's all her imaginary nursing of my digestive system, or just that she's better under fire, but Syl marched upstairs and pulled Lizzy together in the process. She found my pulse and set about rubbing my arms and putting warm compresses on my head to increase blood flow or something like that.… Lizzy kept a lookout for my parents, who arrived at six in the morning (after breaking an awful lot of speed limits).

Being a neurologist, my dad is usually pretty stoic at the bedside, but I don't think they were quite prepared for my condition. I was sort of blue by then and cold to the touch; Lizzy told me our mother turned a similar color when she saw me. You have to give them credit, though; they managed to keep up appearances until my aunt was safely sent off to get some rest.

That's when the real panic started. Lizzy gave them a quick rundown of events, explaining that the blood had been stolen by a "vampire-hunting freak," and that I hadn't had a drop since the Sunday before. She pushed aside my torn shirt to show them the red X, and my mother just totally broke down. Lizzy said she was sort of crying over me in a pathetic way and cradling my head. I have to say, I'm sorry to have missed it. (My mother's kind of scary a lot of the time, so this would have been awfully satisfying.) My dad was afraid that force-feeding me would make me choke, so he performed an *actual* transfusion. That would be my second transfusion, as it happens, followed immediately after by my third and my fourth. I started showing signs of life after that, and some color came back into my face. I guess I had a few moments of lucidity here and there during the process, and I managed to get something down the natural way (well, for me, anyhow). All in all, they put more than a week's worth of blood into my body that morning, which meant I had been down to next to none when they started. Apparently, without fresh blood coming in, my body stops making or maintaining its own. That's one to log away for future use, I think.

It was Monday before I was up and around, and Lizzy, who refused to return to camp, was hanging around like one of the Velcro cats. I'd spent the morning drawing X's through my notepad sketches of Zsòfia and the afternoon reading *Sports Illustrated* in bed. Lizzy was lying across the foot of it playing solitaire on Mom's phone. Suddenly, she gave me sharp look.

"It's kind of ironic, isn't it?" she asked. The look on her face suggested we'd been having a deep conversation, except that she hadn't included me.

"I have no idea what you're talking about."

"Well, you almost died," she began.

"And that's ironic?"

"No, stupid. You didn't let me finish," Ah, I was stupid again. Honeymoon's over. "You almost died from not eating because for you, not eating is like bleeding to death on the inside. That's ironic."

"Why?" I asked. Clearly I missed the significance. She rolled her eyes.

"Think about it, Jake," she continued, "A vampire either sucks out someone's blood, or bleeds to death himself. It's like, you suffer the same fate as the victim, you know?"

"That's a cheerful thought," I said. I'd had enough blood and death for one summer and didn't need that kind of visual.

"Sorry—but think about it.... What a script that would be."

"Lizzy, I don't *want* to think about it," I said. "And I don't want to be in one of your plays, thanks." She shrugged and bounced off my bed and toward the door.

"Suit yourself—it was probably my finest role," she said grinning.

And for once, I had to agree.

"Hey Liz," I started. I wanted to say a lot of things, you know, about bravery and loyalty and brains and mad acting skills, but it's my sister so I just said "Thanks. Thanks for being the cavalry."

"You're welcome—and next time, don't be so dumb."

I winked and traced an X over my chest.

"Stake my heart and hope to die," I said, and Lizzy hit me with a pillow. She never appreciates my sense of humor—but that's drama queens for you.

About the Author

A SCHOLAR OF MEDICAL-HUMANITIES AND WRITER OF Gothic fiction, Dr. Brandy Schillace spends her time in the mist-shrouded alleyways between medical history and literature. She is the Managing Editor, *Culture, Medicine and Psychiatry* and Research Associate/Guest Curator for Dittrick Museum. Dr. Schillace is a freelance writer for magazines and blogs, and has published fiction as well as non-fiction books (*Death's Summer Coat*, Elliott and Thompson, 2015).

About Cooperative Press

COOPERATIVE PRESS (FORMERLY ANEZKA MEDIA) WAS founded in 2007 by Shannon Okey, a voracious reader as well as writer and editor, who had been doing freelance acquisitions work, introducing authors with projects she believed in to editors at various publishers.

Although working with traditional publishers can be very rewarding, there are some books that fly under their radar. They're too avant-garde, or the marketing department doesn't know how to sell them, or they don't think they'll sell 50,000 copies in a year.

5,000 or 50,000. Does the book matter to that 5,000? Then it should be published.

In 2009, Cooperative Press changed its named to reflect the relationships we have developed with authors working on books. We work together to put out the best quality books we can and share in the proceeds accordingly.

Thank you for supporting independent publishers and authors.

WWW.COOPERATIVEPRESS.COM

CPSIA information can be obtained at www.ICGtesting.com
Printed in the USA
BVOW07s1226050814

361434BV00002B/9/P